WHITE MAGIC

WHITE MAGIC

SPELLS TO HOLD YOU

A NOVEL

KELLY EASTON

Published by Wendy Lamb Books
an imprint of Random House Children's Books
a division of Random House, Inc.
New York

Wendy Lamb Books and colophon are trademarks of Random House, Inc.

www.randomhouse.com/teens

Educators and librarians, for a variety of teaching tools, visit us at
www.randomhouse.com/teachers

Library of Congress Cataloging-in-Publication Data
Easton, Kelly.
White magic : spells to hold you : a novel / Kelly Easton. — 1st ed.
p. cm.
"This novel was originally a play, titled Three witches and a wart, which was first performed at Words and Music Theater, in San Diego."
Summary: Three high school girls in Santa Monica form a coven to try to get what they feel is missing from their lives.
ISBN 978-0-375-83769-2 (trade)—ISBN 978-0-375-93769-9 (GLB)
[1. Witchcraft—Fiction. 2. High schools—Fiction. 3. Schools—Fiction.
4. Friendship—Fiction. 5. Santa Monica (Calif.)—Fiction.] I. Title.
PZ7.E13155Whi 2007
[Fic]—dc22
2006039735

The text of this book is set in 12.5-point Apollo MT.

Book design by Angela Carlino

Printed in the United States of America

10 9 8 7 6 5 4 3 2 1

First Edition

For my witches: Randall Easton Wickham, Joanne Baines, Marilynn Easton, Sheli Easton, Isabelle Easton Spivack, Celia and Katie Wickham.

WHITE MAGIC

CASTING
SPELLS

CHRISSIE

In the beginning was the
word, and the word always
had two syllables: trashcan,
gutter, bubble on the water,
waiting, always knowing,
that it will pop.

Here's something I remember from when I was little. My dad decided we should get a goat. He'd been in Tibet designing a system to draw water up a craggy mountain to a small village.

The Tibetans used the goats for meat and milk and to carry things. One time, my dad woke up and a goat was lying next to him in his tent, eating his sleeping bag. He laughed so much, he woke everyone up at the camp.

So when he came home, we drove over to a farm. I picked the first goat that walked up to us. It was white and cross-eyed. Vermonters have a reputation for not saying much. The farmer lived up to it. He took Dad's fifty bucks and went back into his house. Dad and I tied the rope around the goat and tugged her to the car. I sat in the backseat of the old Mustang with her. "Keep her still," Dad instructed, which made us both crack up, because we knew it was impossible.

I called the goat Wilbur, after the pig in *Charlotte's Web*. "But it's a girl," my mom complained when we got home. "You can't call a girl Wilbur. Besides, it's not a pig."

"Chrissie has poetic license," Dad said.

Poetic license. The phrase stuck with me even though he hasn't. It means you can do whatever you want with words.

"Chrissie!" My mom doesn't knock anymore. It's one of those things she's shed since we moved to California last week, like her brown hair and cooking meals. "Why are you just sitting here? Why don't you do something?"

"There's nothing to do here."

"Unpack, for goodness' sake."

"I don't feel like it."

"Write in your poetry notebook."

"I just did. My poem sucks."

"Don't say 'sucks.' "

"My poem stinks."

"I'm sure it's fantastic. Why don't you read it to me?"

"I want to read it to Mr. Credenzo and see what he thinks."

"E-mail it to him."

"I'm not his student anymore."

"He'd love to hear from you and you know it."

I can't argue with that; my last day of class, he made me swear I'd send him poems. So I change the subject. "I want to hang out with Jason."

"Call him, then."

"Calling is not hanging out, especially when the person is your best friend your whole life and he lives across the country. Besides, he's not home. And don't tell me to e-mail because I IM'd him twice and he didn't answer."

"Okay. Instead of pining away for Jason, maybe you need to make new friends."

"How?"

"There must be kids you'll like at your new school. Just smile at them and be terribly friendly. They won't be able to resist."

The words *terribly* plus *friendly* sum it up. I do friendly terribly. Mom does it well. Even glaring at me, she's charming. Like Ava Gardner, the old movie star she was named after. "Did you notice that people don't wear clothes here? I mean, there's a girl in my English class who wore a jog bra to school. How can I smile at someone who's half naked?"

"They dress that way because it's hot. If we were in Vermont right now, I'd be shivering and you'd be shoveling snow. Look at that sunshine flowing through your window."

"It hurts my eyes."

"You're making me very tired. Do you know that?"

"It's that bleach they put on your hair. Bad chemicals. They permeate the skin."

"These are highlights. Nothing *permeated* anywhere. Help me unload groceries, Chrissie, since you're not doing anything else. I bought a ton of food."

"You mean we're not eating takeout?"

"Give me a break. I just unpacked the dishes."

I follow her down to the kitchen. Every wall in our new condo is white. No wallpaper. Just white. The staircase is Plexiglas. You can see through it. And it has no banister, nothing to guide you on the stairs; a person's got to have a guide. "Someday I'm going to fall off of this thing and crack my head open." There is no way I'm making this easy for her.

"You don't fall off the stairs when you're fifteen."

In Vermont, our house was two hundred years old. The banister had carvings of angels, their features made smooth by two hundred years of loving hands. "Why do we have to live so close to the beach? If there's an earthquake, we'll be swallowed up by a tidal wave or monsoon. I read that California is slipping into the ocean."

"That will take centuries." Mom sighs. "Most kids would love to live near the beach."

"Why did we have to move here?"

Mom slings a bag at me. "Because I have been invited to work at the best advertising agency in the country."

"You could've kept working from your computer at home!"

"I never wanted to live like that, out there in the woods with no one to talk to. Freezing nine months out of the year. Your dad wanted it that way, but now . . ."

"What?"

"I couldn't stay there. Not without him. And you, sitting there on the porch day after day, waiting . . ."

She doesn't finish, but I know what she means. Waiting for him to come back. It's what I did. Same as when he was alive and would drive in from town.

"Besides, Max was getting tired of a long-distance relationship. . . ."

Mind Occupation: my own invention. It's a way of blocking out what I don't want to hear. So while Mom goes on about the virtues of her boyfriend, Max, I take myself back to Vermont. There's still snow in March. Jason and I go sledding; then we take the horses out for exercise.

"Are you listening?" Mom holds up a cauliflower as if it's a severed head.

"Not really."

"Fine!" She puts her hands on her hips, which means a lecture is coming, with maybe a bit of yelling for decoration. Luckily, her cell phone rings (for the fiftieth time today). She dashes upstairs to answer. I hear her Max voice, sweet as taffy. "Darling, how was the meeting?" She never called my dad *darling*; she called him by his name, Peter, or Pete, if she was cranky.

I go to the front door and peer outside. March, and it's eighty-five degrees. The palm trees on our street look like upended brooms. They definitely belong on a movie set. Even the light in L.A. seems fake, brightly slicing through the air like a knife.

I grab Mom's Dior shades off the table, step outside, and tug the door closed behind me.

There's a sidewalk, but no one else is on foot. Like the song: "Walking in L.A. Nobody walks in L.A." But I do. I walk past a row of snazzy condos like ours, through an even ritzier neighborhood, away from the beach past Crow's Sporting Goods, Jane's Juice, Phat Boys and Fitness Freaks, Remax, Cramer's One-Hour Liposuction, GloryWorld Tanning Salon, and 7-11, then into a part of town that changes to beat-up apartments.

Hopefully, Mom will be so busy talking to "Darling" that she won't notice I've flown the coop.

Mom used to have pet names for me. Candy names like Tootsie and Sweet Tart. She called me that when she told me we were going to move, that her boss, Max, had promoted her and she needed to be in L.A. I remember that moment like people remember a car crash or a tornado. My speechlessness. She was so apologetic; she knew she was trading my happiness for hers. "I'll do anything to make this work for you. I promise." Now she's impatient with my misery. And while she blossoms, I wilt.

I check my watch. I've been walking thirty minutes. I stop and turn back for home and then I see it, a sign drawn with a black marker like some kid's made it. And it says:

Aura Analyses, Psychic Readings, Phrenology, Tarot, Palmistry, Crystal Ball, Channeling, Wicca, Dowsing, Telepathy, Homeopathy, and Raising of the Dead

YVONNE

SPELL TO CALL A LOST
MOTHER TO YOU

Sprinkle feathers, mint leaves, sugar, and cinnamon into a brass bowl. Take any objects associated with the missing person and place them in a circle on the floor. Light a candle in your window to attract the spirit children. For two moons, turn to the east. For two moons, turn to the north, saying: "Come now, mother. Come back to me. I call to the forest. I call to the sea. I call to the earth mother, come back to me."

★ ★ ★

Every house has its noises. I imagine them to be the dead and invisible souls come to life in objects. The silverware rattles in its drawer, the curtains swish, the walls groan. My dad's snores sound like a herd of elephants.

In England, there are ley lines, mystical gaps in the landscape where time and space disappear. Children have vanished within these lines. When the parents search for them, they can still hear their children's voices. The police arrive. They comb the area. But they cannot find them and, in time, the voices become like the lick of a river against the shore. Just part of the landscape.

When I can't sleep at night, it's the fault of the noise. It's like part of me is lost within a ley line, slipped into the gap of time and space. If I listen hard enough, I can hear my past.

I came to L.A. from Italy when I was only six. Before that, I lived in a caravan with a group of Gypsies. My dad says that during the day, my mom took me into the city to beg. Whatever city we were near: Milan, Florence, Rome, I would beg; my hands cupped into a bowl, my eyes wide and pleading.

But I don't remember this. What I remember are the campsites in the evening: children dangling like fruit from the trees; toddlers wading naked in the stream; old ladies in long dresses chanting incantations; men strumming guitars.

My dad says it was no life for me, no life for a child. He wanted greatness for me in the world. He didn't want me to beg. He had a brother here in Santa Monica with a beach stand that sold hot dogs. He thought this was a good opportunity ("This is your idea of greatness?" I nag him, when he bugs me about cleaning my room).

My dad is half Gypsy, half German. The German half wanted order and was tired of moving from place to place and being treated like "the scum of the earth."

So, deep in the night while my Gypsy-mom slept, my dad stole me and fled to Calais, France, then to England. From there, we flew to the New World.

I don't know how he managed it all, but we became U.S. citizens. The land of opportunity, he said.

At first, I worked at the hot dog stand with my dad and helped cook the food. I would walk in and pull the fries out of the freezer, stack the cups. Then my dad would cook the hot dogs, but the smell of the meat would make me puke.

Do you know what's in hot dogs? Organs, brains, ground-up bones, nitrates, corn syrup, the parts of dead animals that usually get thrown in the trash. Might as well toss in a pinch of mad cow or bird flu.

Don't eat a hot dog. This is my advice to you.

So my dad had to send me to school while he was at work. I liked school: the wooden desks, the pages of the books like dried leaves. I was given a reader. It was so old that part of the *F* had rubbed off of the title, making it look like a *T*. My first year at school, I thought America was the Land of the Tree. I considered that a nice idea.

I quickly learned to read, and other things: how to mumble a spell and ace a test, how to make a clock run faster. If kids laughed at my accent or my ugly clothes, I made voodoo pictures. I drew Jorge Garcia with a bowl of soup on his head. That day, he slipped in the cafeteria and landed in someone's lunch. I drew snotty Betsy Carol with blood coming from her arm. The next day, she got a staple in her hand.

I began to realize my powers.

What I hadn't yet learned was that my mom was one of the best witches among the Gypsies, and that magic was coursing through at least half of my blood. Nor had I realized the laws of karma; that a hateful spell catapults through the universe like an echo in a canyon, returning in full force to its sender. Whatever I did to someone else, something twice as bad would happen to me. Right after the Jorge spell, my uncle left for Mexico and we never saw him again. After Betsy Carol, I broke my ankle jumping rope.

In fourth grade, we moved from East L.A. to Santa Monica. I was so taken with the ocean, the pull of it like a magnet to my blood.

My first day at my new school, a blond girl entered the class in front of me. When she went to sit down, a boy stuck out his leg and tripped her. She took the whole desk down with her as she fell. Everybody in the class laughed and pointed, except me.

All day, kids made fun of the girl. It was clearly an old habit with them, but I couldn't figure out why. She was pretty and had cute clothes. She seemed nice. But I guess it just takes one person; meanness is a contagious disease. You can just look at history to figure that out. One person decides to oppress another and others will follow along like sheep.

Every time someone called her *stupid* or *lame-o* my heart felt like a watermelon smashed on the pavement, even though I knew I was lucky it wasn't me.

That night, when I went home, I did a spell *for* her. It was fairly simple. I crushed some flower petals and held them to my lips, then wished her safe from harm. But there was such *intention* in that spell. A spell only works in relation to your intention. It was the first time I'd done a spell *for* someone, rather than *against* someone.

Five minutes later, there was a knock on the door and the karma of my spell began to work. It was the apartment building's owner. He offered my dad a job as manager, which meant our apartment would be free. To celebrate, my dad took me shopping for new clothes. I was wandering through the aisles of Target when I saw her, the blond girl from class. She was standing like a statue with a box of shoes in her hand. "Here." She walked over to me. "These will look nice on you."

The shoes were red sandals with sequins. They

weren't something I would normally wear. "Ruby slippers," I joked. I slid them on. They looked great. "Don't you want them?"

"I only like white."

I wiggled my toes. "They're perfect; good witch shoes. I'm kind of a witch." I had never told anyone in my life.

"Can I be one too?"

"Sure," I said. It was that easy.

The next day, when we walked into class, the boy tried to trip her. This time, I brought my ruby slipper down hard on his foot. "Try that again and I'll turn you into a worm."

It was so much easier to stick up for her than for myself.

After that, me and Karen were pretty much left alone. She is the closest person to me, aside from my dad, and my mom, who I only meet in dreams, when the noises blur and I finally fall asleep. Then she comes. Mom has hair like black wool and skin like satin, and she sings me lullabies.

When I ask my dad about my mom he says she had gray hair, wrinkled skin, and a black cavern for a mouth, that she used me as a slave and her voice was harsh. But I know that she is the woman in my dreams, and that her voice is beautiful.

All of this is going through my mind today, as I go to the bathroom, stare at my face in the mirror, wash my hands, throw my dad's *Sports Illustrated* swimsuit issue into the trash, and see, through the window, a prospective customer. Sometimes when I look at someone, I get an immediate gut feeling.

Sometimes, I don't. It's what sucks about intuition; it's unpredictable. This girl is tall and kind of gawky with short brown hair. And I do get an immediate feeling: pain.

CHRISSIE

So this sign appears. I stop and look at it. Then a girl runs out of one of the apartments, dancing with bare feet on the hot pavement. "Can I help you?" The girl has black hair to her waist. "You were looking at my sign." Her makeup is so heavy, it's hard to tell if she's thirteen or thirty. Her eyes are lined in black and there's gold glitter on her lids. She looks kind of Goth, but also pretty. "Nice shades," she says.

I try to think of something to reply. *I'll just be moving along now. See ya.*

She's staring at me, the way I might examine a cell mutation under a microscope. "Black cat got your tongue?"

"What is phrenology?" I finally ask.

"Reading the bumps on the head."

"Oh. Now I remember."

"Everyone remembers once you tell them," she says, but not meanly. "The sign's pretty dated. I'm out of the ingredients for some things. Like raising the dead. That takes saffron, which is expensive." She cocks her head like she's listening. "Is that what you wanted? For me to raise the dead?"

Boom! A faucet switches on and water pours from my eyes.

"Don't worry. It's okay," the girl says. "You're just not yourself today. Come inside and we'll fix you up." She sounds like a mom so I follow her into apartment 6. Someone has drawn two other sixes so it says 666, the sign of the devil.

Again, she reads my mind. "One of the idiots who lives here wrote that. My name is Yvonne. I'm not a devil, just a witch."

I follow her into a dark apartment and try not to think of this book I read, *Helter Skelter,* about an L.A. cult in the sixties run by Charles Manson, who broke into a house and murdered everyone, even a pregnant woman. When my mom saw me reading the book, she took it from me and threw it in the trash. What would she say if she knew I was going into a stranger's apartment, a strange stranger? A *witch*?

The door seems to blow closed behind me, although

there isn't any wind. Inside, the only thing I can make out is a light under a door and two round balls glowing in space.

"Karen! Someone is here," Yvonne calls.

"Is it Jimmy?" comes a small voice.

"No! Why would it be Jimmy?" Yvonne whispers to me, "Karen has a major thing for Jimmy."

"Only since September," the voice says. "Turn on the lights, Yvonne. I can't even see her."

Yvonne flips on the lights. The apartment appears: a beat-up tweed couch with a blanket thrown over it, a vinyl easy chair, a TV. The floating balls are cat eyes and the cat, naturally, is black. "That's Wizard," Yvonne says. "He's my familiar."

Karen is about my age, pretty, blond, and petite, like most of the girls in Santa Monica. She's wearing a white sundress and white sandals.

"We were asking the Ouija board about Jimmy," Karen says, "but it wouldn't say if he liked me. Your eyes are really puffy. Have you tried frozen cucumbers?"

"I was crying," I say, and only then do I notice that I've stopped.

Karen comes closer. She seems cautious. "Why were you crying?"

"Just . . ." I blink.

"Sad?"

I nod. "I just moved here."

"Oh. That's hard."

"I'll make some tea," Yvonne says. Only a counter divides the kitchen from the small living room. Wherever she goes, the black cat follows. Yvonne puts a kettle on.

"Who's Jimmy?" I ask, to get the attention off me.

"He's this boy at school," Karen says.

"There's always a boy," Yvonne adds.

"I hadn't even noticed Jimmy until the first day of school." Karen gets a dreamy look on her face. "My backpack broke and my books spilled. Everyone around me was laughing and I felt like I was in a play, you know, where you can't remember your lines."

"Yeah, I know that feeling." I feel that way all the time since we moved here.

"Then Jimmy bent over and picked up all my books, my pencils, my ruler, and handed them back to me. It was so sweet."

"They're always sweet until you get to know them," Yvonne says.

"He's a senior."

The kettle whistles. Yvonne pours hot water into cups and brings them into the living room on a tray. "Mint tea is calming."

As we sip tea, I tell them about our move, Vermont, even a little about my dad's death. It's weird, telling personal things to strangers; makes me realize how isolated I've been.

Yvonne watches me like she's trying to decide something. Finally, she says, "We have a coven of witches. But don't worry. We only do white magic."

Karen looks startled.

Yvonne tilts her head. "Maybe you'd like to join."

KAREN

YVONNE'S SPELL TO ATTRACT A BOY

Take five of the finest hairs from the head of the beloved. Combine this with five of your own. Using mint and crushed hyacinth bulb, create a tincture to be placed on the pulse points of the body. Kneel and recite: "Amorous, Giver, Suffer, Olorious. Bring my lover and make him glorious." (Sometimes love is not meant to be; if this is the case, even his whole head of hair will not help.)

22

I have Jimmy's hair. At night, after everyone is asleep, I place the strands in the cup of my palm and examine every thread.

Jimmy's hair is dark blond. I would never use the phrase *dirty blond* for Jimmy's hair. *Dirty* is a dirty word. He should wash it more often, though. Sometimes when I see him at school, his hair is so greasy that it's stuck to his head. But he lives in a car, so I forgive him. I will always forgive him, because that is what love is. Still, I'd like to give him a bottle of Herbal Essences, just as a hint.

You can tell a lot from a single strand of hair: vitamin deficiencies, drug use. Hair lasts after you die. That is because it is already dead.

I never let any escape to the floor where I might step on it. I don't want my foot to be on Jimmy. You don't step on people you love.

Reasons why Jimmy should love me:
1. Because I have his hair and have recited over 200 spells.
2. Because I'm naturally blond and petite.
3. Because I am neat and tidy. I shower every day, wipe the toilet after peeing, brush my teeth after every meal, and iron my clothes.
4. Because Yvonne said he will, and she is the head priestess, the only other witch until today when Yvonne let a COMPLETE STRANGER into our

coven. But it's okay because now we'll have more power, she says.

5. Because I love him. He's all I think about. I want to be his shirt, tugged over his shoulders and buttoned up. I would even be the collar or cuffs.

Reasons why he might not love me:

1. Because I'm not very cool. I get nervous and say the wrong thing. My hands sweat.

2. Because I've made mistakes and thought boys have liked me, then let them do too much with me. Now everyone thinks I'm a slut.

3. Because people think that my head is like a bubble-gum dispenser, just a few colored balls clanking around in there, dropping out for a penny.

4. Because my only friend is Yvonne, although lately Gina Sorino talks to me in P.E. She goes, "Karen, your eyes are pretty. You should be on TV. There's like a casting call at Fox, I read. Why don't you audition?" Or "Where'd you get that peasant top? You really look like a peasant."

Mom says the world is my seashell, my box of chocolates. I can savor the beauty and sweetness.

But life has always felt more like a rough ocean than a shell, tossing me in the waves, making me feel good one moment and awful the next.

It's the other kids. I've always been out of synch

with them. In the kindergarten play, we did the can-can dance. While all the girls kicked left, I kicked right. When we played circle games, my hands were sweaty, so no one wanted to hold them. At my communion, I choked on the wafer and spat it out on the priest. I raised my hand in class, but then couldn't remember the answer. In third grade, when Derek Garner told me his dad was a Vietnam vet, I thought he meant he worked with animals, and everyone laughed. I'm also gullible. When Eddie Reynolds said he wouldn't tell if I let him put his hand under my shirt, I believed him. When Corey Willis said he loved me, I believed him. And the other boys—I believed them all. Yvonne's the only one I can really trust. And my mom.

The new witch's name is Chrissie. She just moved from Vermont and she hates it here. She goes, "There's seasons and covered bridges and snow!" Then she goes, "L.A. seems a little unreal." I thought that was weird. *Unreal*. I've never been anywhere else but here. What could be more real than California? Movie stars live here.

Chrissie's smart in that way where she doesn't worry about being pretty. She's got short brown hair, freckles like a kid, and round owly glasses. She's tall and kind of beefy without being fat. She's a nerd, maybe, but I like her even if I'm not sure she should join our coven. Why should we need a third member after all these years? But Yvonne said she had a feeling. This is a dark age, a dark time. Three is a powerful number. So . . . *whatever.*

Chrissie was nice, actually. When I told her about my love for Jimmy, she nodded like I was talking about an important painting or a piece of history and she was studying it.

Yvonne said, "Tell us about your pain." And Chrissie went, "My dad fell off a pipe into a river in India."

"India!" I said. "That is too weird. Did he, like, die?"

Chrissie nodded.

Yvonne kind of gave me a dirty look, which made me feel bad. "Did he drown, or did he die from the impact?"

Chrissie didn't answer the question, but I guess it doesn't matter, 'cause dead is dead.

"What was he doing on a pipe?" I asked. "Why would anyone be on a pipe in India?"

"He was making clean water for people." Chrissie lowered her head, so that I could barely hear her.

"That is so scary, Chrissie. One day he's there, and the next he's not."

"Everything is scary to Karen," Yvonne explained, which I didn't think was a nice thing to say, but it's true. Yvonne tells the truth. That's all there is to being a witch. Seeing what is really true, the things that no one else notices. And telling the truth.

Scared. Yeah, that's me.

Maybe it's because of my dark streak. At church, one time, I tasted the holy water instead of making the sign of the cross, because, well, I'd run the whole way there and I was thirsty. Another time I smuggled a candle home in my dress so I could pray alone. The priest said to have no idols before you, but I have boys. I'm boy-crazy and always have been. I even liked Jay Angorra, who tried to trip me for years and got everyone making fun of me, something that still happens to this day.

I go home for dinner. "What did you and Yvonne do today?" My mom smiles.

"Studied," I go, which is a sort of lie. We *did* study spells.

At dinner, Mom dishes out gobs of potatoes, peas and beets. She still cuts my meat for me.

She wants me to be eight years old and to stay that way.

I wish I could.

Mom talks about her favorite movie, *My Fair Lady*, and how Eliza Doolittle is made over by Henry Higgins. There should be more people like Henry Higgins, she says, to make over all those terrorists and suicide bombers. All those people who think there's only one road, without realizing that a road can branch and grow in different directions, like toward the light.

And Dad goes, "Uh-huh." He says that a lot because his mind is a planet in space.

But my mom doesn't care. She has her house, her child, her cozy relationship with God.

She doesn't know the way my heart, like a piece of china, has been chipped over the years by one wrong boy after another. (Jimmy is the right one. Finally.)

"Karen," she goes, "would you like some apple crumble? Dad? Apple crumble?"

"Sure," Dad says, writing numbers on a piece of paper, because he's an accountant and there's always something to add or subtract. "Nothing like your apple crumble."

"No thanks," I go. I wish I didn't have to always watch my weight.

Later, I call Jimmy. Usually, his dad answers (I hope he doesn't have caller I.D.). But, if I'm lucky, for ten seconds, I'll hear Jimmy's voice: "Hello, hello, hello . . ."

I want to speak, but it's like I've swallowed a Big Mac in one piece and it's stuck in my throat.

"To hell with you!" Jimmy finally yells into the receiver, because he doesn't know it's me. By then it's too late to say anything.

Click. He hangs up. The phone is a dead bird in my hand.

I go to my room, cry, then put on my Barbie pajamas. I kneel. My rosary slips through my fingers, but instead of saying "Hail Mary," I go, "Hail Jimmy," knowing that it's a sin, but thinking that if God can forgive a repentant murderer who makes a last-minute confession, then He can forgive me, because I am just a dumb teenager after all. Besides, I'll probably go to hell for being a witch (even though Yvonne says I won't).

When I go to tell my dad goodnight, that boy is there, the one who's helping him fix up the house. He says, "Wanna watch the game?" He's in college. His name is Troy. He gets more attention from my dad than I do, I swear.

"Sports are boring."

"Not if you eat a bunch of good stuff." Troy holds up a can of Pringles.

"Karen hates sports. She and her mom both," Dad says.

"What *do* you like?" Troy asks, which seems kind of fresh. Besides, it's hard to find an answer.

"Tennis," I say, because I once took lessons. *Witches.* "Swimming in the ocean. I like that."

"You surf?"

"No. I want to be *in* the ocean, not on top of it."

He smiles like I've said something funny, but at least he doesn't laugh at me. "I know what you mean. My dad used to send me to sailing camp every year and I hated it. I just wanted to dive off the boat into the water."

"Look at that play!" Dad says. Troy flips his head toward the screen.

A boy who needs to make friends with a dad is

a loser, even if he does have big brown eyes and curly hair.

So I go in the kitchen and help my mom do the dishes. I can't help having a couple of spoonfuls of apple crumble. Mom kisses me goodnight and says, "Sweet Karen."

And I say, "Sweet Mommy," like I have since I can remember.

I love my mom so much. If I disappointed her, I'd kill myself. I really would.

CHRISSIE

Why do we say the sun
rises, when it's the world
that moves? Why do we say
the moon is half, when we
just see it that way?

Language is a broken vase.
Words are the pieces, each
syllable a piece of glass.
Even glued together, you
can see the cracks.

I'm a member of a coven. What next? How could things possibly get any weirder? I entered a stranger's home, spilled my guts like I was in therapy, then pricked my finger and let the blood drip over a white candle. "What actually *is* a coven?" I asked.

"The word actually means a meeting," Yvonne told me. "We are a group, meeting for a sacred purpose."

I sat in a chair and closed my eyes and they did these chants. I felt a little nervous, but also relaxed for the first time since I moved here.

After, Yvonne brought out the Ouija board and Karen asked all these questions about Jimmy. The pointer moved so fast, spelling out words, that I could barely keep up with it. When Karen asked if Jimmy loved her, it shot to the word *yes*. It was obvious Yvonne was controlling it.

After, they told me about themselves, and how they've had their coven since, like, fourth grade and I'm the first person they ever invited to join it. Then Yvonne gave me this speech about the rules. She goes: "To be a witch is to listen to your inner voice, to be in tune with nature, and to notice synchronicity. That's a meaningful coincidence, like two people thinking the same thing at the same time. Or knowing who it is when the phone rings. To be a witch is also to cast spells. That's very important. A spell is a kind of prayer."

"Tell her the rules," Karen said.

"The rules: You are not allowed to use drugs. Drugs are like running a race on broken legs and not knowing it. You are not allowed to smoke, because I can't stand the smell of cigarettes. I made my dad quit too. It was very hard on him. Alcohol is okay, but only one glass of wine or a beer. Being drunk takes away your power. Go easy on technology. Turn off your cell phone before meetings. We try to talk on the phone to each other instead of e-mailing; it's too impersonal. Limit all forms of media and technology, because it removes you from nature. You are not allowed to blog. When you blog, you give yourself away, your most private details, for cheap, for free. Have faith. If you have the right intention, the universe will take care of you. Our coven is secret. You can tell people you're a witch, but not about the coven. Secret is sacred."

She didn't need to worry about that. I'd hardly be telling people that I'm a witch, let alone belong to a coven. Not that I know anyone. Still, I nodded. *I have friends,* I kept thinking. For the first time since I got here, I felt a bit at home. I wanted to stay longer, but all of a sudden, it was twilight. I practically ran out of there, leaving behind Mom's Dior shades.

Now, it's taken me about an hour to find my way home. I made a wrong turn at Phat Boys and Fitness Freaks and I'm crossing my fingers that Mom's gone out. But no, there's another car in the driveway, a snazzy Porsche. Max! Only he would drive such a pretentious car.

The whole condo is lit up, head to toe. My dad

used to conserve energy. He installed solar panels and put in a wood-burning stove. He was so aware of how much waste there is in this country and how little others had. Before he married my mom, he lived in Nepal and India. He actually met Mother Teresa.

The front of our house is all windows, so I creep around the side and sneak between the hibiscus plants to the back door, thinking maybe I can pretend I was upstairs. I tiptoe through the hall and check my cell phone; twelve missed calls and all from my mom!

"Chrissie! Thank God. Chrissie, get in here."

I stroll into the kitchen like I haven't just checked out of the house for four hours. "Hi, Mom."

" 'Hi, Mom'? I was just about to call the police and all you can say is 'Hi, Mom'?" A stream of words pours out, about my irresponsibility and changed personality. I haven't seen her this mad since I smuggled Wilbur into our house and he ate her couch. She screamed, but Dad and I laughed hysterically at the sight of the goat lying on the couch munching on the upholstery. "Do you ever even think how your actions might affect me?"

Mind Occupation: My mom is dressed up in a black evening gown. She's wearing a diamond necklace with a ruby *A* hanging from it. It's not the kind of necklace my dad would've given her; that's for sure. He went in for turquoise, beads and shells he found on Cape Cod.

Max wears a tuxedo. He is tall, maybe six-two, and tan. He looks like an aging actor, Harrison Ford or maybe Clint Eastwood. I've met him only twice before we moved, when he visited us in Vermont. At that point, I didn't realize he was such a threat. Each time he came, he brought me an expensive gift: a blue suede jacket that remains in the box to this day, and a cashmere sweater with real pearls on the collar that also remains in the box. Mom made elaborate dinners when he came, like she was this Suzy Homemaker. That should have tipped me off.

Then there were all the trips she took out here. She called them business trips. I got to stay with Jason and his big family, their dogs and horses, so I didn't mind. When Mom was away, Jason and I would sneak into my house and hang out like we were grown-ups with our own place. I remember once, we crawled out of my bedroom window and sat on the roof ledge tossing white pebbles into the trees, watching the moon glint off them like they were fireflies.

"Don't you ever . . . ," Mom goes on.

I take myself to Yvonne's apartment, her instructions about what I'm supposed to collect in order to join the coven: a pearl, three strands of Mom's hair, six strands of mine, a postage stamp from a precious letter, the thread from an important hem.

But Mom's words keep getting through: "Worried sick, thoughtless teenager, endangering your life . . ." At least she didn't notice the missing shades.

"Shouldn't we get a chance to reacquaint?" Max finally interrupts. He has the nerve to be smiling at me, like this is a nice family scene rather than me being yelled at.

Mom shakes her highlighted hair, cute as Meg Ryan. "Well, I guess."

"It's so nice to see you again, Chrissie." He holds out a manicured hand. But I don't shake it. "You've grown about six inches since I last saw you."

Yeah, it's great to be four inches taller than anyone else in your school.

Mom glares at me. "Chrissie."

I touch his hand with one finger, then withdraw it. "Nice to see you, too." My voice stiff.

"How are you enjoying sunny California? Isn't it a relief to be away from the snow?"

"No."

"Chrissie!"

"I like snow."

"Where were you?" Mom taps her foot.

"I went for a walk."

"For four hours? Without your cell phone?"

"Oh yeah, my phone. I just wanted to see what's around here. You know? Explore the terrain, like I did every day in *Vermont*."

"This isn't Vermont!"

"No kidding," I say, but mildly. I really don't need to get her any madder.

Max pulls out a glass from the cupboard. *Like he lives here!* And it occurs to me, all of a sudden, that Mom never could've bought a condo like this on her

36

own. Never. Max bought it. He owns it. Owns us. He fills the glass with water.

"We have a very important engagement. Because of you, we're late."

Another night alone. I should've stayed with Yvonne and Karen.

Max hands the glass of water to me. Loser! I don't want anything from him. But then my throat's gone all deserty.

"The fridge is full. I'm sure you can fend for yourself," Mom says.

The water is cloudy. Microorganisms. Bacteria.

"Can I have bottled water?" I ask.

"Sure thing." Max opens *our* fridge, pulls out a Perrier and pours it into the glass, then adds ice. "The only kind we have is with gas. I hope that's okay."

The look I give him makes Mom giggle. "That's what they say in Europe, Chrissie. 'Gas' means carbonated."

"Oh."

"What do you say?" Mom prods.

"Thank you." All of a sudden, I feel like I'm going to cry again. I turn and rush upstairs, but even in my room with its overpriced walls I can hear them discussing me, the specimen: *Adolescent. Stage. Adjustment. Hormones.*

You gotta love being reduced to hormones.

I grab my pen and pull out my journal, try to use my anger for a poem, but my tears turn the ink into puddles.

JIMMY

I'm on a cliff. A . . . precipice. That's the word. The earth is falling apart beneath my feet. The earth's crust, crumbling like a cookie. This dude comes. He looks like Eminem. Mean. Pierced eyebrow. He's Eminem but he's got my dad's voice. He tries to push me off the cliff. I wrestle with him, but he's stronger. He holds me over the water, ready to let go of me. "Say the word," he goes, "and I won't drop you."

I open my mouth to speak. But my stutter is back. I can only get out the first letter. "P-p-p . . ."

"Last chance," he goes.

"D-d-d-o-o . . ."

"You can't even save yourself." He tosses me over the edge.

I fall, but I don't die. I just splat onto the water, my body in pieces like a Mr. Potato Head toy. My arm is stuck on the bank. My head floats down the river. How can I see my own head floating if I'm not wearing it?

The howl of sirens wakes me, or maybe it's the sun turning the car into a sauna. I should've left the windows open.

"I'm awake," I say out loud, to remind myself it's just a dream. And I don't stutter. My mom spent a bunch of money we didn't have on speech therapy, then drilled me every night for years until I talked in one piece. Chicks love that. A smooth talker.

When I sit up my knee hits the steering wheel of the piece-of-shit MG. I was so psyched when my dad bought it. But then he said, "If you decide to tie one on, this is where you're sleeping. Don't even set foot in the house."

Maybe that's why Mom left; my dad's habit of laying things out in black and white, of drawing lines you're not allowed to cross. Too many years in the military. And we're all soldiers, right, ready to salute. That's probably why he likes working with plants so much. Line them up in a row, water them, and they'll do just what you say.

At first, I lived with Mom. We made meals together

at night, watched shows like any family. But then I got drunk one night and took a baseball bat to the TV. The Dodgers had lost yet again, and I was pissed.

"I can't do this with you," she told me. "Make a new start." Like life was something from a recipe and I was the wrong ingredient. She was going to AA twice a day and working at a nursery school. Isn't it funny? Dad owns a nursery and Mom works in a nursery. Plants and kids.

I try to check the time, but my watch is smashed. How did I do that? I reach for my phone, but it's not in my pocket. Must've gotten drunker than I meant to last night. My license is suspended so I'm grounded, gonna have to hoof it. If I'm late one more time, I'm gonna be suspended. I got to graduate. If I do, my mom'll think I'm on track. She'll know I'm not stuck repeating the same shit over and over, like some kind of jumpy CD.

The guidance counselor tells me to have goals. Goal #1. Stop saying *shit* so much. Stop *thinking* it. You are what you think. Think shit. Be shit. Goal # 2. Stop drinking. In the morning, hung over, it seems easy to achieve, but . . .

My head is pounding. My legs are stiff as I step out of the car. The houses are identical in this neighborhood. But inside, they must be different. If I step into another house, will I have a different life? At the end of the street, a flashing light: a cop car or an ambulance.

Does someone old live there? Are they being carted away? Or did some kid overdose? Don't know my neighbors except Slab, my bud since first grade.

I've been in an ambulance once, passenger-style, after a fight I got into at a party. I'd walked into the night air to sober up and found a knife in my side. It was plugged in there good, just a bit of blood creeping out, like the Halloween stuff my mom dripped from my vampire teeth when I was little.

Slab came out after me, bragging about the damage done to the other guy. I don't even remember who it was.

"Looky here." I lifted my arms like some kind of dancer. I was so drunk I thought it was funny. A knife stuck in my side.

In the ambulance, I was treated like a king. The EMT was a woman, a kid with freckles. I said, "Am I going to die?" and she held my hand, asked me questions: Where did I grow up? Did I have a girlfriend, and if so, was she pretty?

"Iraq," I said, wanting to say something nice, but it came out mean. "The girls at my school are dogs."

She dropped my hand, and I figured it out then. No matter how much I wanted to do something right, I was always going to screw up.

You are what you think.

House unlocked. And only 7:30 a.m. I can make it to school. Luck. Luck. Luck. But I won't have time to shower.

Dad already gone. Work ethic man. But the house is so messy. Dust everywhere. A pillow and blanket on the couch, so my dad slept with the TV. The photograph of my mom, the one good picture of her, holding her little dog and smiling into the camera, is facedown.

I'm dying of thirst. Dehydrated. It's the booze. Open the fridge. Nada except a couple of beers. A beer won't hurt. Smooth the day. Ease the hangover. Quench the thirst.

The radio news says there's a drought. In San Diego, a commemoration of some school shooting. Columbine, was it? No. That was Colorado. La Mesa?

Think pleasant thoughts.

The phone rings. I run over. But the portable's not on the charger. The ringing is coming from upstairs. The machine picks up.

"Jimmy. Uh, hi. This is Yvonne Cionesco. I know this sounds weird, but do you mind stopping by this afternoon? I want to talk to you."

Yvonne! With the long black hair and a body like a *Playboy* pinup, if she'd only wear something reasonable instead of that Goth crap. I search for a pen to write down the address.

Yvonne. I can't believe it. Does she like me? Maybe? Why else would she want to see me? She's the most beautiful girl in school, and a guy can talk to her. A guy can say hi, and she'll say hi back.

A guy can fall in love.

CHRISSIE

The ocean is a forest of
water. The forest is a tree
in a house of mirrors. A
tree is a stick giving
direction to the wind.

Meet the room. Everything about it nautical. A canopy bed with pale green mosquito netting, like sea foam. A round window; a portal. Light blue walls. There's even a painting of a beach with seashells, like something you might find in a doctor's office.

Then there's the sound. Once Mom and Max stop talking and laughing . . . once the cars with their massive speakers stop driving by . . . once the neighbor's TV stops blasting sports . . . I can hear it: the sound of the surf, the water, the sea. The word used to describe waves is *crashing*. As in, the tidal wave crashed into the village, killing all of the inhabitants. As in, the man's body crashed into the water.

Is it possible to have seasickness on land?

Don't sleep. It's as simple as that. Don't be caught off guard, and carried away by the Pacific Ocean, with its smell of salt spray and fish, which seems much more insidious than the Atlantic.

But I do sleep, eventually. And that's the problem. I fall asleep around four o'clock, and dream of tidal waves and sinking ships: the *Lusitania*, the *Titanic*. Then, at six, when the alarm blasts like a foghorn, I'm exhausted.

Still, I get up. What else can I do? I've never missed a day of school in my life, except when I had chicken pox, although if I did miss at this school no one would notice because I'm invisible. A zero out of six hundred students.

My school in Vermont had two hundred kids, total, kindergarten through high school, and we all knew each other. I only remember one kid moving away. Ever.

When I was little, I rode to school on the back of Dad's bike. Then, when I was older, we rode together. Sometimes, just for fun, Jason's dad hitched the horses to the wagon and took us. Dad was good friends with

Jason's dad. They loved to ride around in that horse and wagon. Both of them were into nature and conservation. My mom's idea of conservation is using less mascara.

When my dad was on trips, I felt like I was holding my breath. I still did the normal things. I skied, rode horses, hung out, but part of me was suspended.

That's what I was dreaming about when the alarm went off: riding horses with Jason. We were searching the woods for my dad. But then Jason was gone too. In his place was a woman wearing a mask, like a bandit from an old Western. I reached over and pulled off the mask, but there was no face there.

I woke myself up then, snapped out of the nightmare. And when I went back to sleep I dreamed well, of snow. The paper-white, laundry-clean smell of it. The bite of it on my face. A climate where it's perfectly respectable to have pale skin and to wear beat-up sweaters and jeans.

Usually, I start a pot of coffee for Mom, but not today. I'm not doing anything for her. Last night, she came home all excited and happy, wearing a giant diamond ring on her left hand. At first, she didn't say anything about it, just kept going on and on about some ad campaign she's working on for Dane's Pantyhose. The ad has four Great Danes, standing on their hind legs wearing the panty hose. The copy says: THERE IS NOTHING LIKE A DANE.

I thought it was pretty clever, actually, but I said, "Yeah, most women want to compare themselves to dogs."

"I'm sure you'd design it with goats." She tried to make a joke, but I could tell she was hurt.

"What's with Mount Everest on your hand?" My throat was so tight I thought I couldn't breathe.

"Oh." She blushed. "I was going to tell you. Max and I are engaged."

It isn't enough that he practically lives here, and that I had to be yanked out of my life like a weed by its roots. I should've expected this, like everything else. A guy doesn't buy a million-dollar condominium for someone he's just going to date. I'm sure it's something they planned all along and are trying to feed to me, like mashed fruit to a baby, one spoon at a time.

"I know it's a big change, Chrissie, but it's been three years."

I didn't give her a chance to finish. I turned on her and darted upstairs, into my sea room, and locked the door. She didn't follow. Later, I heard Max's car drive up, his footsteps, his voice. She tried to lure me from my room with dinner, but I wouldn't open the door, so she left a tray outside, like room service. I would've liked to boycott the food, but I was starving.

All night, they talked and laughed. Dishes clattered. A bottle of champagne was opened. Pop!

And now, worse, his car is still in the driveway. He spent the night! I should ground her. They're not married yet. I should sneak a group of boys into *my* room (if only there were boys who would come), have a party with drugs and alcohol and cigarettes. I should steal the keys to Max's little red Porsche and crash it.

But no. I'm responsible and reasonable, my dad's daughter.

It's half an hour before I have to leave, but I do not want to run into them. So I grab a five from the money drawer (yes, the *money* drawer!) and walk to school instead of busing it, stop at Java the Hut for a double cappuccino to get me through the long, lonely school day.

I make my way through English, which I hate. Yesterday, the teacher, Ms. Chin, made us write a poem using two lines with three verbs and three adjectives, as if poetry is a formula, a science. She's nothing like Mr. Credenzo, who had us reading e. e. cummings and Adrienne Rich and Hart Crane, and taught us to play with language like it was paint and we were applying it to canvas.

Today is worse. We're filling in our own adjectives to someone else's pathetic poem. The author's name isn't even on the page. And everything has to rhyme.

We have block periods, which are killer when you have a bad teacher, an hour and a half of misinformation about poetry. I sleep with my eyes open (not a bad line for a poem!).

Biology is better, although I much prefer chemistry,

the transformation of one thing to another (again, my dad's daughter). The teacher's name is Stoner. I figured it was a joke at first, but it's really his name. Today we're supposed to take a quiz on genetics, but this girl, Gina Sorino, asks so many questions that the time is disappearing. "Why did they call the cloned sheep Dolly, if that wasn't the first sheep's name? If they cloned George Bush would this one start wars?"

My lab partner is pretty nice. His name is Sam and he's the only person in the school who has bothered to talk to me. He asked me where I was from and how I liked it here. When I said I didn't, he said, "Yeah, California's like its own soulless country." Which I thought was a pretty cool thing to say. He's a little nerdy, with carrot hair, and glasses taped in the middle but also cute and really buff. He must play some sport.

My first day, when I was stressing over a quiz question on a subject I'd never studied, his hand slid over and he tapped the right answer. Which was nice, but unnecessary. I'm sure I could have figured it out on my own. Anyway, he shares the invisibility factor with me. The couple of times I saw him between classes, he was by himself.

He also draws cartoons of the people in the class, exaggerating their features like those artists at fairs. I figure I'll try to find him at lunch today, maybe start a conversation about the human genome, the ethics of tissue research, deep-tissue massage, tissue paper, *whatever*. Just to have someone to talk to!

When class is over, I walk out. One of the jocks hands Gina a dollar, so I guess the question stuff is an act. This school is so weird. I try to follow Sam, but the halls are crowded and I lose sight of him.

The cafeteria is packed with kids. I'm pretty sure they're breaking some kind of fire code. I search for the carrot hair, but don't see him, so I look for anywhere to just squeeze in; there is nothing more embarrassing than eating lunch by yourself. Nothing.

There's a crowd around one table. As I get closer, I see the first happy thing since I've moved here. Yvonne, the witch, eyes closed, hair spilling over her shoulders like a shawl, sits in front of a giant marble. Propped on her head are my mom's shades.

"Chrissie!" Karen waves at me. "Look, Yvonne, it's Chrissie!"

Yvonne opens her eyes, interrupts her trance or whatever, and stares at me. So does everyone else. I make my way through the bodies and sit down.

"Didn't I tell you she'd be in school here?" Yvonne gloats.

"You did," Karen says. "Of course you did."

"I brought you your sunglasses." Yvonne pulls them reluctantly off her head.

"Keep them," I offer, stupidly. *Just don't ever wear them in front of my mom,* I want to add.

"Thanks." She smiles. From the looks of her apartment, I don't think she's ever owned Dior anything.

"Okay, break it up," Stoner calls. "All you anorexics return to your tables and eat your lunches."

The crowd parts. And only then do I notice that no one else is *sitting* at our table; it's just me and Karen and Yvonne. "Everyone's scared of me," Yvonne explains, reading my mind; it's weird how she can do that.

"What were you doing?" I ask.

"Sports readings." Yvonne yawns. "Boring, but it keeps them entertained, and me fed." She gestures to the offerings on the table: a Coke, a banana, a package of Oreos and a granola bar.

"Chrissie," Karen whispers. "Look behind you. Standing up. That's Jimmy. Tell me if you don't think he's awesome!" A boy with brown spiky hair, a pierced nose, and a Linkin Park T-shirt holds up the wall with his skinny frame. He's good-looking in a bad-boy way. "That's Jimmy?"

"Thrilling, huh?" Yvonne says.

"Shhh," Karen scolds. "He's to die for."

"Meet at the bottom of the stairs after school," Yvonne says, "and we'll start the preparations for your entrance into the coven."

I guess the blood-over-the-candle routine was just the start. But I don't care, so long as I have friends. "Sure."

After lunch, I walk to my locker, feeling happier

than I have since I moved here. Yvonne and Karen aren't in A.P. so we don't have classes together, but at least I won't be alone at lunch. It takes me a couple of times to remember my combination. A group of kids comes by. One of them, a girl who looks like a pop star wannabe, shoves up against me deliberately.

"So *sorry*," she mocks. "Don't put a spell on me."

"Witch!" another girl taunts.

"Freakette," Wannabe says.

I am no longer invisible.

YVONNE

SPELL TO WARD OFF WARTS

Take one leaf of eucalyptus, one leaf of magnolia. Soak overnight in six tablespoons of witch hazel and one of lavender oil. In the morning cover the affected area with the leaves. Leave on for six hours or more, if necessary. Allow no oxygen to reach the affected area, no feeling to reach your heart.

I see several different visions when I close my eyes. It's like my mind is a computer, and screen savers appear. One is a tower built of granite, stones and shells. The top of it is crumbling, as if it could fall anytime. A tower is temenos, a meeting place with God or spirit. My tower is broken because the bridge between my past and present has been severed. I'm reaching into the universe, asking for guidance. But while I can guide others, there's no path for me. It's like calling directory assistance for your own number and finding there's no one listed by that name.

At seven o'clock, Jimmy comes to my house, an hour late. He's dressed up for once, with a button-down shirt and cords. Jimmy always has this startled look, like a kid walking into his own surprise party. His hair is spiked on his head. If he let it be normal, soft, he'd actually be good-looking. He smells like beer, cigarettes and some kind of cheap aftershave.

"You're late," I tell him. "I asked you to come at six."

"That happens to me a lot."

"What happens to you?"

"I'm late."

"Being late isn't something that *happens* to you. It's something you do."

"Sure feels like it happens to me. Like time slows down just when I'm trying to speed up. I couldn't believe it that you called me." He takes out a cigarette.

"No smoking."

He puts the cigarette back. "One of my many bad habits."

"I bet you think habits happen to you too."

He smiles. I've never seen him smile before. His smile is huge and his teeth are white, for a smoker.

"Sit here."

He plops down at my round table and stares at all the objects on the red tasseled cloth: my crystal ball, my tarot cards, my candles and incense, my sacred stones.

"That's the thing you always bring to school." He points at the crystal ball.

"Hold out your hand."

He stretches his hand toward me.

"Palm up. You're not here for a manicure!"

"What *am* I here for?"

I don't like the way that sounds so I ignore him and focus on the webbed lines of his palm. "Your palm is like an eighty-year-old's."

"Yeah?"

"You've lived way too hard. Your love line is a shambles. Your life line is cut up in five pieces."

"Does that mean I'll die five times?"

"Death is metaphoric. Get it? Changing schools is a death. Being a teenager is the death of your childhood."

"Wow. You say such cool things. 'Death is metaphoric.' " He closes his hand around mine. "Your hands are soft."

All of a sudden, I realize that having a rough boy over when I'm by myself is kind of a bad idea. I yank my hand away. "That's not the point."

"What is the point? You called me. Usually when a girl calls a guy and invites him over, there's a point. You know what I mean?"

"Are you drunk?"

"Nah, I just had a beer with Slab. Just one beer . . . maybe two. Three, tops."

"Slab. That guy's aura is black! I'd stay away from Slab if I were you."

"What's an aura?"

"It's the light that circles your body."

"Like in those pictures of Jesus? There's a gold light around his head."

"Right. Like that. Gold and white are the highest colors, the purest. Okay, we'll use the cards."

"Your lips are really red. Like flowers. Do you wear lipstick?"

"No."

"You're so pretty."

"Touch the backs of the ones that draw you to them, them I'll turn them over."

He touches the cards. "I like the palm reading better."

I turn them over. "This card is eyeball . . . which means vision. This one is ice cream cone, which means innocence, although the ice cream can fall off, plop onto the sidewalk, which means loss of innocence. Juggler; that's obvious."

"Where'd you get those cards? Those are cool."

"The Bodhi Tree, but I had to special-order them."

"It's like you're in another world. Like there's another world than high school."

"There *is* another world than high school. Try to concentrate."

"That's always been my problem. I can't concentrate. ADHD. For anything unpleasant they use abbreviations. You ever notice that?"

I didn't expect Jimmy to be so honest. Direct. It takes me aback. "The interpretation of the cards changes over time. You put them in the present context. Next year, they might mean something totally different."

"What does that have to do with me?"

"Everything has everything to do with everyone. A person sneezing in China can affect the price of gas here."

"See, you say shit like that. No one else says shit like that."

"I do not say . . . shit."

"Sorry. Is that why gas is so high? Someone sneezed in China?" He laughs.

"I was just making a point. Gas is high because the President is sleeping with the Saudis."

"Sleeping?"

"It's a figure of speech."

"You're, like, hot *and* smart."

"You know who's smart? Karen is smart. That's who's smart. Now let me concentrate." I turn the cards.

I don't want to tell him this, but they do not look great. "Closed book. You should read more. Gagged woman. Not sure what that means. Broken heart. Do you have any questions?"

"What do the rest mean?"

"Judge with no face; not sure yet. Cowboy hat means George Bush or Dick Cheney and war, war, war. Male brutality. Privilege. Imperialism. Don't get me started on that. Do you have a problem being too macho, trying to create some stereotype of being a man?"

"I don't think so. My dad does, though, definitely. He's military."

"That's bad."

"Yeah, it's like a religion. You know? Nothing can compare to it. No one is as important."

"Not even you?" I ask. To my dad, I am the most important thing.

"Nah."

The way he looks down makes me feel sad. That's what happens when someone feels too much; they look away. "Sorry."

"It doesn't matter." He tries to smile.

Something tugs in me, like a tide pulled back into the ocean by the moon. "The cards are promising something new in your life. Let's look at the crystal ball."

"Something new?" He sounds hopeful. "I guess you're something new."

"It doesn't mean me. If it meant me, I would know."

"Will you go out with me Friday night?"

I shove the ball toward him. "Look in there. Do you see what I see?"

"I don't see anything."

"I see something." I rub the ball. "Wow, this is so cool."

"What do you see?"

"Luck."

"Luck?" He snorts. "I wouldn't know luck if it bit me on the ass." He folds his arms. Folded arms. Closed door.

"Did anyone ever tell you you have a way with words?"

"No."

"They won't. Trust me."

He shrugs. "So what's so lucky?"

"A beautiful blonde. She is five foot seven, has blue eyes, beautiful tan legs and white sandals."

"Is it you?"

"Do I have blond hair and blue eyes? Duh!"

"Who is it, then?"

"It's a little foggy yet. I'm trying to see. This girl is awesome. And full of love. She is what you need."

"I'll tell you what I need," he says. "A spell."

"A spell?"

"I heard you do spells."

"For what?"

"To bring my mom back, and to hold on to her."

"Your mom?"

"She flew the coop. She wanted to do this . . . makeover of her life. She stopped drinking, got a new job, joined a gym. She's got a boyfriend with a ponytail. And my dad. Well, he's never been the most cheerful guy, but now he's miserable. And I . . . I just miss my mom." His voice cracks a little. Against my will, feeling wells up in me.

"My mom's gone too."

"Really?" he says, touching my hand, but like a friend, like he understands. It makes me kind of see why Karen likes him.

"Are you an only child?"

"Uh-huh."

"That makes four of us."

"There's only two that matter, as far as I can tell." He slides his hand around mine, tugs me toward him.

I yank my hand away. "Let's talk about the girl."

"You?"

"No, not *me*. Blond. Blond!"

"I don't like blondes. Listen, Godsmack is coming to town. My friend Meth works at Ticketmaster. He can score tickets to anything."

"I hate that band. It's like listening to car crashes."

"Who do you like?"

"Billie Holiday."

"Who's he?"

"She! She sings the blues. She's the best."

"Well, I'll go online and find out where she's playing. I'll get tickets and we can go!"

"She's dead!"

"We'll do something else. You name it."

"No."

"You called *me*, you know, and I thought, *Yvonne is the coolest chick I know, and she's calling me!* And I felt like my luck was really changing."

"Most of the kids don't think I'm too cool."

"They do, man. They're just a little scared of you. They think you're a witch."

"Duh! I *am* a witch."

"Let's make out. Just a little. Then I'll know my luck has changed."

Make out? What charm. "Look in the crystal ball."

"Yeah. What, now?"

"See anything?"

"You and me making out."

"No! That isn't what you see! What you see is a cute blond girl. That's what's there. And if you don't see that, you're blind."

He pushes back his chair and stands up. "I get it. It's your friend. That chick you hang around with. The one who wears white. You're trying to fix me up with her."

"Karen," I say. "Could you wish for anyone prettier?"

"She follows me around wherever I go, then hides when I look at her, like she's some kind of a nutcase. The other day, she comes up behind me, says 'Hold still,' then cuts off a piece of my hair."

"Hair is powerful."

60

"She calls my house . . ."

"She is the sweetest person in the world. And you are an idiot if you don't like her."

"I like *you*!" he says.

The way he says it, combined with the fact that we are both missing our moms, makes my stomach go funny. Jimmy has big eyes and a wide face. If it wasn't for his piercings and spiky hair, he would be downright handsome. "I'm not in the cards, uh, crystal."

"Nothing I want is ever in the cards. It's like you're dying for an ice cream and just when you get there the store closes. You go to the pool and they've drained the water. You know what I mean?"

"That will all change if you're with Karen."

"You want me to love Karen?"

"It's your fate. It has nothing to do with what I want."

"Then *you* love *me*." The scent of beer from his breath wafts toward me. He lunges at me.

On the spot, I make up a distancing spell: "Yibba, yabba, don'ta grabba." For good measure, I shove him as hard as I can.

He falls. The back of his head hits the wall.

"Ow. What did you do to me?"

"Nothing," I say. "Just a spell."

"You really are a witch."

"That's right. I'm a witch and you're a wart."

I hear my dad's key turning in the lock. I can do just about anything I want except have boys in the house. "My dad's here." I open the window. "Jump out."

"I wanna meet your dad."

"If you don't climb out the window, he'll throw you out."

"I'll be back."

"Not unless you go out with Karen."

"What do I get out of it?"

"Karen! Duh."

"I want a kiss."

"Vonny!" I hear my dad's voice.

"Go!"

"A kiss."

"All right." I kiss his cheek.

Jimmy pushes the loose screen and climbs out. He falls to the ground with a thud. I wonder if anything's broken, but he jumps up and scurries away. He's completely under my power.

"Vonny." Dad barges into my room. "Did I hear a male voice?"

"Since when did knocking go out of style?"

"I heard a boy's voice!" Now he's almost yelling.

I cannot lie to my dad. "It was Jimmy. I made him go out the window."

"Who's Jimmy?"

"Just a boy from school."

"I don't want boys in here."

"I know."

"I don't trust boys. I've told you that." Now he's totally yelling.

"Okay."

"I've been a boy. None of them are up to any good."

"Point made. Can you lower your voice before you pop my eardrums?"

"What kind of boy jumps out of the window? I ask you that. Instead of shaking my hand and leaving through the front door."

"I told him to."

"What were you doing with him?"

"Nothing. Karen likes him."

"Don't I give you freedom? With freedom comes responsibility." My dad has a thick accent. His huge black mustache is a hedge over his mouth and teeth. I've often wanted to tell him that his mustache is the reason he never gets a date, but I don't have the heart. I've tried numerous spells to make it fall off, but even magic has its limits.

"It won't happen again. *Okay?*"

"Want some rice?" He finally gets the point.

"And broccoli."

"I'll start the water, then I just have to check a toilet in four A."

"Okay, I'll put the rice in when the water boils."

"How was your day?"

"Fine," I say, but I'm feeling a bit unsettled, my stomach fluttery, my mind in knots. "How 'bout you?"

"I think people are getting weirder than ever. This

woman comes to the window and says she wants her hot dogs *married*. I had no idea what she meant. Turns out she wants two wieners on one bun. Crazy. This is the kind of day I have, so I don't need surprises."

"No surprises."

"Let's go out. I should be spending more time with you."

"Cool." It's been a while since my dad and I have gone anyplace.

"The Classic has a *Star Wars* marathon."

"Again?"

"It always calms me."

We go to see *Star Wars* for the millionth time. I think my dad likes it because there's a good force and a bad force and the good force comes out on top. He wants to think that's how the world works. Of course, I know that each and every one of us has both forces within and they're battling all the time, like a little *Star Wars* in our bodies. A tibia for a fibula, a rib for an eye, bone fighting bone and brain wrestling with heart.

CHRISSIE

Am I fat?" Karen looks at herself in the mirror. "Maybe I'm getting fat."

"You're so pretty," I say. "You're not fat."

"I should spend more time chewing my bites," Karen says. "My mom said Laura Bush keeps her weight down by chewing every bite thirty-nine times."

Yvonne frowns. "Who wants to look like Laura Bush?"

"Imagine," I say, "foreign dignitaries talking with her about world peace. And she'd be going 'Twenty-nine, thirty . . .' "

"I think it was Nancy Reagan who counted her bites," Yvonne says. "Remember Nancy Reagan?"

"We weren't even born yet," Karen says.

"How come it's always the Republicans who are such bad actors?" I say. "Like Ronald Reagan and Charlton Heston . . ."

"And Arnold Schwarzenegger," Yvonne snorts. "The worst."

"My parents are Republicans." Karen looks insulted.

"Yes, but we love you anyway." Yvonne sprinkles herbs in a bowl of water, lights candles and incense. "Did you bring everything?"

"Yeah." I offer her the bag.

"The M&M's are just to eat. Life isn't life without chocolate. They don't write about chocolate in any of the spell books or Wiccan tracts that I've read, but in my spell book, chocolate plays a major part."

"Did you write the spells in that big black book?" I ask.

"Yeah, or adapted them from other spells." Yvonne holds up a bag of M&M's.

"I want the blue ones." Karen pounces. "I love blue. My mom thinks I like pink. She gets me all these pink Barbie things, and I hate Barbie. I hate pink."

"Just tell her," Yvonne says.

"Sounds like she doesn't want you to grow up." I hand a blue to Karen.

"She doesn't. It's true. And when I have kids, I won't want them to grow up. And I don't want *us* to grow up."

"I'm to a thirty-six C," Yvonne jokes, "so I am definitely growing up, or *out*."

"At least you have a letter," I say. "I'm not even *A* yet. It doesn't seem fair to be big everywhere but there!"

"You look good, Chrissie," Yvonne says. "Just as you are."

"Since I've had a thing for Jimmy, I've lost five pounds," Karen says.

"You can have the blues if you forget about Jimmy." Yvonne rattles the bag.

"The Ouija board said he loves me! Now you say I should forget him!"

"You can do better. That's all. That boy who always hangs around your house? What's his name?"

"Troy? He's so full of himself. My mom asked him what he's majoring in and he goes 'premed.' Since when is that a major?"

"It's an intention," Yvonne says. "And it means he's smart. That's what it means."

"He's a loser. His only friend is my dad."

"How do you know that? You only see him at your house."

"What did you think of him?" Karen asks me. "Did you think he was cute?"

My mom and Max were meeting with the wedding planner last night, which made me want to barf, so I hid out with Karen. Her mom was as sweet as Karen is. Her dad hardly said anything, but Troy was hot:

brown curly hair, big blue eyes. He reminded me of Jason a little, that same outdoors look. I tried to get Troy's attention by asking about UCLA. He answered my questions politely, but his eyes, literally, never left Karen. "I thought he was gorgeous. Kind of like Brad Pitt with curls."

"And glasses. I hate glasses." Karen blushes. "No offense, Chrissie. I mean, on boys. You look great with glasses. He talks about epidemiology. I don't even know what that means."

"It's the study of diseases," I say.

"Creepy."

"Okay. Fine," Yvonne says. "We'll keep working on Jimmy."

"Good," Karen agrees.

"What color M&M do you like, Chrissie?" Yvonne hands me the bag.

"It doesn't matter. They all taste the same. Oh, I meant to ask you. Who is that girl at school with really blond hair and heavy makeup? She's kind of chunky and she drives a black Mercedes and wears the highest heels I've ever seen."

"Is she mean?" Karen asks.

"Yeah," I say. "She's always pulling stuff on me. It's totally random. Like, she put an egg in my backpack and it got all over my stuff; now the pages of my books stick together, and they smell really bad. Then the other day, my clothes disappeared from my gym locker and I had to wear my gym clothes the rest of the day. I don't know how she got into my locker."

"Trish Vandevere," Karen says.

"Definitely." Yvonne narrows her eyes. "She gets away with whatever she wants, because her dad is always causing a stink."

"Trish doesn't do anything to me," Karen says. "She just calls *me* a slut. She says it like it's my name, like it's nothing. Like, 'Can I borrow your pen, *slut.*' Gina said she's mean because her dad won't let her have a nose job until she's eighteen."

"Trish is bugging you because of us," Yvonne says.

"Let's put a spell on her." Karen grins. "What's the spell for turning someone into a toad?"

"Getama, Salona, Reptiva, Toad." Yvonne waves her hands like a magician.

"Does it really work?" I ask, knowing that it doesn't.

"Nah"—Yvonne shakes her head—"although it can bring bad luck. It's symbolic. Internal. It names them what they are inside, although she's really more of a snake. *Getama, Salona, Reptiva, Toad.*"

"*Getama, Salona, Reptiva, Toad,*" I repeat. "I've never had anyone . . . make fun of me."

"You get used to it," Yvonne says, which makes me feel bad for her. She's pretty weird. She's probably been made fun of her whole life.

"I just don't fit in here."

"You mean you can fit in one place, but not another? I just thought either you do or you don't," Karen says.

"I fit in in Vermont."

"Who wants to fit in?" Yvonne frowns.

"Have you seen that reality TV show called *The Swan*?" Karen asks. "I always wonder about that, whether it's possible to re-create yourself, to just choose who you are, like buying a dress."

"This is the place for it," I say. "I've never seen so many plastic surgery advertisements in my life. Even on the front page of the newspaper!"

"I really don't *get* reality TV," Yvonne muses. "Reality is so . . . boring. And it's all that's on."

"There's always been reality TV," I joke. "*National Geographic.*"

"I *hate* those nature shows," Karen says. "Some lion pouncing on a deer, *murdering* it."

"I wouldn't exactly call it murder." Yvonne strokes Wizard. "The lion is just eating dinner. People are the only ones who murder just for the heck of it."

"My dad loved that show," I say. It's the first time I've really talked much about him to anyone in three years. "And he loved the Science Channel and Animal Planet."

"You must miss him so much," Karen says.

I nod; words won't come.

"Okay." Yvonne takes a deep breath. "We need to dress. Every witch connects herself with a color.

70

Karen is white because she's pure, aside from a few lapses, and I wear red because I'm vibrant. What color are you?"

"I guess I'm blue," I say, because I mostly wear jeans, because I am *blue*.

"How about this?" Yvonne pulls out of her closet a pale blue silk robe decorated with lilacs.

"Wow, that's beautiful."

"I got it at a thrift shop on Sepulveda. We should all go there sometime."

Karen pulls a flowing white muslin dress over her head. "Now that I'm dressed I have to pee." She dashes to the bathroom.

Yvonne has another Japanese robe for herself. It's red with a dragon on the back. "In terms of being a witch, there's lots to learn, but that takes time. What we were talking about before? *The Swan*. Well, a witch can transform herself, but not in someone else's image. And we're a coven, so we take care of each other." Yvonne steps closer to whisper. "We especially need to take care of Karen and keep her out of trouble."

"Why is she so boy-crazy?"

"I don't know. She's just . . . always been. Maybe she was born that way. Her mom is totally focused on her dad, too, so maybe she learned it. And she always chooses the wrong boy. It drives me crazy. I just try to keep her distracted."

Karen comes back. "Did you tell her about the animal familiar?"

"An animal familiar is the animal you identify with," Yvonne says. "It's very important to your witch identity. Mine is the cat, for obvious reasons."

"Mine is the dolphin," says Karen.

"I'm guessing, Chrissie," Yvonne says, "that yours might be a bird of some kind. Like an owl, which symbolizes wisdom and guidance. Or maybe a crow. You don't have to figure it out, though. It will come to you."

Karen pulls out a red ceramic bowl and puts it in the middle of a small table.

"We'll put most of the ingredients in here." Yvonne looks at me. "Thread from a hem, your mom's hair, the old matchbook, the stamp, the pearl. Did you find a pearl?"

"Yeah, but it's freshwater." Taking things of my mom's is becoming quite a habit.

"That's okay." She puts in my "ingredients," then lights a white candle in the middle. She and Karen recite: "Binding, binding, unwinding and winding, pull together, never apart, the aspect best described as heart."

"Next is the Three Corners Ceremony." Yvonne leads me to a corner of the room.

"It used to be two corners," Karen says, "before you came."

"Breathe deeply, and just follow along."

"Okay," I say, trying to be cool about this weird stuff; the finger-pricking was enough fun for me.

Yvonne stands in one corner, Karen in the other. I try to mimic the dancelike movements of their arms. Yvonne and Karen are graceful, but I probably look like a football player in a ballet class.

"In the spirit of the Gypsies," Yvonne says, "in the spirit of witches of the ages, we call to the powers that be. A single thought has the ability to transform reality. A prayer can change the world. Now repeat after me. We are the witches of the sea . . ."

"What?" I say.

Yvonne looks annoyed at the interruption; she takes this so seriously. "We are the witches of the sea . . ."

"It's the name of our coven," Karen says.

"Oh. Okay." I giggle, nervous. "Just so long as we don't have to go in the ocean or anything."

"Of course we do," Yvonne says, "but not until the water gets warmer, around May."

"Oh."

"What wrong?" Karen says.

"I'm afraid of water," I confess.

"But the ocean is so amazing, Chrissie," Karen says. "It's cleansing and healing. You'll love it."

"I won't."

"You're not kidding about this?" Yvonne tilts her head. Her long black hair falls to one side. "You moved to Santa Monica and you don't like the beach?"

"It wasn't my choice to move here!" My voice comes out angry.

"Does she have to go in?" Karen asks.

"Absolutely," Yvonne says. "She has to *immerse* herself, totally. It's part of the final initiation. We'll just walk at the beach each day, for starters, until the water warms up. The ocean will call to you. Don't worry."

"I'm worried."

"Starting tomorrow, we'll meet at the beach. Now repeat! We are the witches of the sea."

We repeat.

"Our mermaid souls persuade immortality."

Can immortality be *persuaded*? I wonder, but I say, "Our mermaid souls persuade immortality."

"Like plankton, we nourish life in the world."

"Like plankton, we nourish life in the world."

"Like water, we flow and continue."

We finish the chant.

I'm already feeling nauseated about the water, even though May is a few weeks away. Then Yvonne says, "Let's raise your dad," and out of the fun of the evening comes the sudden flash of the funeral: my mom sobbing in her sister Cherry's arms, my dad's parents sitting stone-faced like the stoic New Englanders they are, my own inability to cry or even speak, the casket closed because it had taken so long for us to get him back from the Indian government.

I couldn't look at the coffin. Instead, I stared at the pew in front of me, where someone had carved *I'm Bored* into the wood.

★   ★   ★

74

I want to yell "*No!*" to the séance, to the ocean, to being a witch. But Yvonne's face is so intent, so serious, and they are my only friends in this whole state. So I don't say anything. What difference does it make, anyway? It's all a sham. My dad won't rise from the dead. Didn't I stay up every night, sleepwalking through my days? Didn't I stare at the sky like he would parachute out of it? But

He

Never

Came

Back.

Karen pulls me to the small round table. Yvonne lights three more red candles, then turns out the lights. We hold hands in the circle.

Karen and Yvonne close their eyes. But I leave my eyes open.

"Come, air, come, light, come, candle, come, flame," Yvonne says, dramatically. "Come, spirits into our gentle presence. Your grace is a present."

"Your grace," Karen echoes. She squeezes my hand.

"Ohhhhmm," Yvonne intones. "I feel the spirit."

"I feel . . ." Karen quivers like the flame.

My dad's face comes into my mind, but not smiling like he usually was. He's worried, like when he talked about the places he worked where children were malnourished, dehydrated, where women had to walk miles to carry a single barrel of water home.

"I feel the spirit," they chant. The table starts to

75

shake. One of the candles flickers and goes out. I peer under the table, try to figure out the trick, but nothing's there. And it's not just the table shaking. A tambourine on the shelf trembles, its small cymbals chiming. The floor itself seems to be moving. Major special effects. A glass falls onto the floor. A picture drops off the wall. This is one angry ghost, definitely not my dad. He always moved softly. He would slip into a room and you wouldn't even know he was there.

The lights flash on. "Get under the door frame, Chrissie!" Karen shrieks. She and Yvonne are huddled in the entrance to the bedroom, Karen puffing on an asthma inhaler.

But I just sit at the table and stare at them, telling myself, *I'm asleep, I'm dreaming,* until it stops and the room is still and calm.

"Your first earthquake!" Karen beams at me, like a mother watching her child learn to walk.

Yvonne grins. "Welcome to California."

CASTING STONES

CHRISSIE

YVONNE'S SPELL TO
RELEASE FEAR

Make a list of everything you are afraid of. Circle each item on the list that really is something to be afraid of. Like spiders: No. Like meanness: Yes. Cut out the real fears and put them in a drawer. These are things to be careful of in life. Then take the other fears, the irrational ones, and shred them into pieces. Dispose of them by water or fire, saying, "Goodbye, fear. I no longer hold you near."

Yvonne gave me a spell for releasing fear and a spell to get into the Vermont Writers Workshop. She copied the first one from this big black book of spells she's written over the years. Her handwriting looks like a seven-year-old's.

I was going to throw the papers away. I feel a little silly playing this witch game. But I put them in my pocket instead. They're gifts, and maybe a spell is a kind of poem.

After school today, Yvonne's dad picked us up in his ancient Ford Pinto. As we stood at the curb together, Trish and her group passed us and called out insults. It's easier to handle when the three of us are together. I wish Yvonne and Karen were in my classes. Trish is in two of them: P.E. and biology. Yvonne gave them the evil eye, which actually quieted them some. I ignored them. Karen studied the sidewalk. Once they passed, she started crying. Yvonne put her arm around her. Karen is so vulnerable. And she really does get a hard time from a lot of people, not just Trish. Leaving lunch, some moron with a mullet made a grunting noise at her. A couple of girls whispered as we passed, but they were looking at her, not me. It's weird. Karen walks around with her eyes on the floor like she's scared someone's gonna bite her. Yvonne says she was made fun of a lot when she was little and it hurt her confidence.

It's hard to figure out why. Karen's parents are really nice and normal. She's so sweet. Why would anyone make fun of her? I guess it's just random, like most violence. Senseless.

As soon as she stepped into the car, Karen started talking happily to Yvonne's dad. It was like she'd never been crying. So at least she bounces back.

Yvonne's dad's name is Igor. He reminds me of a bear. He's big with thick black hair, a bushy mustache and dark eyes that always look sad. If I feel out of place in Southern California, I can only guess what he feels.

It took five minutes to drive to the beach, then twenty minutes to find a parking place, during which Igor mumbled in German. I think he was swearing.

Aside from that, he didn't talk much; he just came up with these one-liners, in his heavy accent. "This day reminds me of an ice cream cone," he said. "Already it's melting into memory."

Yvonne is so close to him. I have to admit it gave me a pang of envy.

"Chrissie has never even been to the beach, Dad," Yvonne said. "Can you believe it?"

"What you don't know you won't miss," he said. Mysterious.

"I miss Jimmy," Karen whispered.

"But what you don't know you can't miss," Yvonne said, "according to my dad."

It's weird, but lately Yvonne has been discouraging Karen about Jimmy. She used to kind of egg her on.

"I will walk behind," Igor said. "Then I won't embarrass you girls."

"You don't embarrass us, Dad."

"If any boys come near you, I will pounce on them. Don't worry."

"*That* just might be embarrassing." Yvonne tugged us both ahead of him.

"Why don't you find a girlfriend, Mr. C.?" Karen looked back at him as we walked.

"Too much trouble." He shrugged. "You have to buy presents for them and flowers. I am saving my money for Vonny to go to college."

"Don't sacrifice on my behalf, Dad," Yvonne teased, "or use me as an excuse for your love life."

Santa Monica Beach was so unreal, like a carnival. There were a mime, a juggler, a guy talking about Jesus and the world ending, and a bunch of Hells Angels types drinking something out of paper bags. And, naturally, lots of tanned people in tiny bathing suits on Rollerblades and skateboards. This one half-naked guy was bench-pressing three hundred pounds. "Hey, Dad, you should get buff like that guy."

"As you teenagers would say, 'Yeah. Right.' "

"Jimmy hangs out down here a lot," Karen said, "with his guy friends. One time I saw them and they were outlining their bodies in chalk, you know, like a crime scene of a murder."

"Charming," Yvonne said.

"I'm just going to step in here." Igor pointed to a surf shop. "Maybe I'll take up surfing. I'd like to look at things from the inside of the wave. If we lose each other, we'll meet at the pier in an hour."

"Okay, Dad." Once he was in the shop, Yvonne and Karen shouted, "Run for it."

I could tell this was an old routine. We ran down the boardwalk like someone was chasing us.

We rode the roller coaster and the Ferris wheel and wandered through a little aquarium under the pier. Then Yvonne insisted we go onto the beach.

I trailed behind them through the sand to the water's edge. Yvonne and Karen rolled up their pants and waded into it. The waves seemed huge.

"Yikes," Karen said. "It's freezing today."

"Come on," Yvonne called to me. "Just dip your feet in." She looked goddesslike with her hair blowing in the wind.

"Karen just said it's freezing."

"But it wakes you up!" Yvonne argued.

"Those waves are huge," I said. "They could knock you over."

"Just a toe, Chrissie." Yvonne is so pushy.

"It's too scary."

"We'll hold on to you," Karen promised.

I ran to the edge and touched the sea foam with the toe of my shoe, then rushed back to the dry sand. "There. I did it."

Igor appeared next to me. "What's a sensible girl like you doing with these nuts?"

"Having fun," I admitted. Yvonne and Karen are almost as much fun as Jason.

When Igor drove me home, he looked at our condo and whistled. "Very nice," he said. "Like Disneyland."

I walked in, and Mom and Max were all dressed up again. "Chrissie," Mom said, "there you are. You said you'd be home fifteen minutes ago."

"Five minutes ago." Max looked at his watch.

"I was at the beach. You told me I should go to the beach."

"When you live here," Max said, "the beach is life."

"What kind of car does that man drive?" Ava, the snob, said. "I'm surprised pieces didn't fall off when he pulled away from the curb."

Max chuckled.

I gave them the most evil glare I could, the *evil eye*, it would be called in witchcraft; I'm learning. "He's a very nice man. He owns a restaurant."

"A hot dog stand," Mom said. "That's what you said before."

"Whatever."

"I'm sorry we're going out again. We have a very important dinner with a big client. Once I get to know your friends better, I'll let them come over when we're out. I promise."

"You know them."

"They've been here once, and the whole time you three were locked in your room, so I hardly even got to

84

talk to them. Jason used to chat with me and ask how I was and tell me what he was doing."

"Jason wasn't allowed in my room. Remember? If you want to move back to Vermont, I'll invite Jason over every day."

"Who's this Jason I always hear about?" Max asked. "Your boyfriend?"

None of your business.

Mom laughed, like the idea of me having a boyfriend was absurd. "He was her best buddy her whole life. The two of them were joined at the hip. He was the dorkiest kid you could imagine, but boy did he grow up to be handsome. Don't you think, Chrissie?"

My stomach flip flopped. "If you like green eyes and a big smile." *Yeah, he's handsome.*

"You should invite him to visit." Max smiled. "We could buy the ticket. No problem."

"He'd hate it here."

"Chrissie," Mom warned.

"He would. There's not a real tree for miles."

Max looked confused by that. I'm sure he thinks palm trees count. "We bought you some Thai food." He pulled containers out of a brown bag. "There's Tom Yum Gai, Pad Thai, chicken satay, curried shrimp, Bee Bong, and spring rolls."

"That could feed a small country."

"Max always does everything all the way," Mom chirped.

Max tries to buy people off, I thought.

Mom pecked me on the cheek. I hate it when she does that; so insincere. "You're getting so tall, Tootsie. Time rushes by whether I want it to or not." Then they were out the door, having done their parenting mini-mum: make sure she's home and feed her.

Now I'm here all by myself, thinking about the day, watching the clock turn circles, trying not to be tempted by the food.

I was never home by myself in Vermont. Mom never went anywhere. She hated driving down the dirt road in the winter; she said it felt like ice-skating on wheels. Town was ten miles away. The only other house near us was Jason's, and she didn't like Jason's mom that much; she said they didn't have anything in common. I guess it was Mom who didn't fit in, there.

Dad was a homebody too, when he was actually *home.* There was always so much to do when he got back from his trips: doors and windows to fix, wood to chop for our stove, Mom's list of fix-its, his garden to tend. It was a different way of life.

Talking about Jason makes me so full of longing. He didn't answer my last three e-mails. At least it's not an outright rejection; he doesn't have Internet at home, or TV. I pick up the phone. Why does my heart pound? I used to be more comfortable with him than with anyone on earth. And why is it always me who calls?

"What's up?" His voice is overly cheerful, like he's make-believing he wants to talk.

"My mom's getting married and we had an earthquake. The first one was bad enough, but then there are these 'aftershocks,' like little earthquakes. You won't believe it, but you actually get kind of used to them. My mom was freaked, though, which is highly satisfying to me."

"I keep reading about stuff happening there, like the earthquakes and wildfires, mudslides and kidnappings. It sure makes Vermont seem boring."

"I could use that kind of boredom. Or sanity. I mean, there are signs for plastic surgery everywhere you go: eye lifts, nose jobs, breast augmentation, liposuction."

"So which is worse? A wedding or an earthquake?"

"A wedding. Definitely. Although, sometimes, earthquakes cause tidal waves. I mean, not this time. The waves were big, though. I went right down to the water and checked it out for myself."

"Yeah?" Then silence.

"With my friends."

"Sounds good."

"Yeah. I guess. I'm applying to the teen writers' workshop in Montpelier," I say, "so maybe I'll be back in Vermont for the summer."

"Cool."

"But I probably won't get in."

"You'll get in."

"What time is it there?"

"Just nine. Chrissie . . ." It sounds like he's about to get me off the phone. He's done that a couple of times; it's like he's always busy. Or maybe he's mad at me for moving.

"How's Wilbur doing?"

"She keeps trying to go to your house."

"Oh God. Don't let her near the river. Okay? If she tries to cross the river, she could drown."

"Chrissie."

"What?"

"She's a goat. She runs free. You know?"

"Yeah. I guess. Hey, remember the time we looked for her for hours and hours, calling and whistling in the woods. Then we discovered that old tree house."

"How could I forget?" He laughs. "It started pouring and we got in the tree house and the roof leaked."

"Wilbur was on the chaise lounge the whole time."

"Yeah, Wilbur is a character. My mom is still scared to death of her. You should see the way she tiptoes around when Wilbur's there, then dashes to her car."

"How's your mom? And your dad? Is his back better?"

"They're fine. Hey, listen, can I call you back later? I've got someone over."

"Oh. *Someone?*"

"Yeah. Remember Glory?"

A girl from the South, like my mom. Morning glory. Closed tight at night. Open in the morning.

"Uhm. Maybe I do."

"Yeah. She's sort of my girlfriend."

Sort of? "Oh."

"So let's talk later. Okay?"

"Yeah, sure."

"You doing all right?"

"Yeah, I'm cool."

"I'll call you later. And don't worry. I'll look out for Wilbur."

"Okay. Thanks."

But he won't call back. He never does. It's like he's forgotten all the years we were best friends and the things we did.

In first grade, we sat next to each other and shared everything: pencils, erasers, candy smuggled from home. In second grade, they bought a new pony, Spencer. The pony was so gentle, we could climb on him together, bareback, and he'd walk carefully around the pen in circles. In fourth grade, we grew the biggest pumpkin together. The prize was a trip to Canobie Lake in New Hampshire. Our dads took us and they got adjoining rooms at the motel. We rode the roller coaster until we couldn't feel our heads on our shoulders anymore. There are so many great things I remember. In sixth grade, we formed a larger group with Bobby Winters and Lori Shipley.

In seventh grade, Jason tried to kiss me, and I

wanted him to, I really did, but I got shy and gave him a joking shove. Now I wished I'd let him. Then maybe he wouldn't be so hot on Morning Glory, because he'd be my boyfriend, and he'd miss me, *Mourning* Glory. He'd miss me like crazy.

I go to the kitchen and open all the containers of food, then load up a plate. I take out Yvonne's spells from my pocket and lay them in front of me. *Spell for getting what you want,* the first one says. *Close your eyes. Focus on your animal familiar.*

My animal. That's right. I'm supposed to figure out what it is. But every time I try to imagine it, I see a seagull soaring over the threatening ocean. That is *so* off base.

KAREN

YVONNE'S SPELL TO BRING HIM TO YOU

By the light of a white candle, close your eyes and recite his name four times, then your own name twice. Open your eyes and see his face in the flame and say: "Bring me to him. Bring him to me. Let our fates be as interwoven as a bird's with its tree."

Who cares about earthquakes? Earthquakes are nothing. The ground doesn't even know it's wreaking havoc. It doesn't care.

There are so many bad things in the world. There are dictators and terrorists and genocide. There are those makeup counter ladies who say they're giving you a free makeover, then won't let you off of the stool until you buy something. There are slaughterhouses. The animals are kept in pens. They are not allowed to move and have to stand in their own poop. There are gases that float into the air and eat away at the thin veil between us and the sun. When the veil is gone, we will all burn up like paper in a flame.

And there are boys who take advantage of girls, like Jay Farrington, who put his hand up my shirt in fifth grade before there was even anything there, and like Matt Farrel, who told me he wouldn't put it inside of me, but just touch, and like . . .

I can't stand to think about it.

When I was little, a blind man lived across the street. His name was Mr. Carson. Every morning at seven o'clock, his front door opened and out he came. He wore a gray suit and hat. He tottered like a penguin with his red-tipped cane. I asked my mom why he moved side to side that way. "He's orienting himself," she said. "He wants to feel for the world around him."

"Where does he go?" I asked.

"He goes to the Center for the Visually Impaired."

"Why do they call it that? Why not say *blind*?"

"To be polite."

"What does he do?"

"I imagine he reads."

"But how?"

"With his fingertips."

Love is like being blind. Touching is Braille.

At first, Yvonne said Jimmy loves me, that he just needs to find himself, or find out for himself.

But now she says I should forget Jimmy. She says he's like slam dancing, exciting at first, but painful later, when your muscles tighten and the bruises throb.

In eight weeks, school will be over and Jimmy will graduate. He could go anywhere then. He could be gone. I'm at the point of desperation.

I wish I was like Chrissie and didn't care about boys! She's so smart. She talks about poetry and what university she'll go to, and what she'll be. A double major, she says: chemistry and creative writing. I can't even think of a single major!

Last night, we had the Second Circle Ceremony, where Chrissie had to tell us about her deepest self. It's the second rite of initiation. I remember when I got to do that and I told Yvonne things that I was embarrassed by and worried about and she just accepted me.

Chrissie said she doesn't want her mom to get married and she doesn't want to go to the wedding. It's like she has no control over her life. Then she talked about important things, like poverty, starvation, dehydration, and AIDS in Africa. It made me feel really dumb.

I don't know. It's like I haven't really thought of a future that is mine, that I could create my life like an artist paints a picture. Nothing becoming something.

All I picture for my future is a boy coming home at night, me making dinner for him, and curling up on the couch together. A life like my mom's. Still, listening to Chrissie made me want to take action and not just do spells and wait for the results.

So I set my alarm for five a.m. I steam my face, put on a mud mask, antiwrinkle cream, sunscreen, base, blush, eyeliner, lipstick, brow mousse, glitter stick and mascara. I paint my finger and toenails, polish my sandals, then I walk the ten blocks to Jimmy's house.

Seeing his MG, I start to have an asthma attack. I puff on my inhaler. It opens my lungs but makes my heart beat even faster.

It's almost light out. Morning happened so gradually, I didn't notice. I tiptoe to the car and peer in.

How cute he looks, all curled up in a sleeping bag, his mouth open like a child, his fists clenched.

I tap on the window. He bolts upright. His eyes are really red and puffy, like mine after I cry. I must admit he doesn't look so hot; this makes him all the more lovable.

He rolls down the window. "What the hell?"

I'll have to work on his potty mouth.

"Wake up, sleepyhead."

"What's going on?"

"I . . ."

"Well, spit it out and let me go back to sleep. I really tied one on last night."

"I really like you." I wanted my voice to come out low and sexy, but I sound like Chucky on *Rugrats*. "I just wanted you to know."

He frowns. "You've been following me around all year. How could I *not* know?"

This isn't how I pictured things going.

"So, do you want to go out or something?"

Jimmy leans back into his sleeping bag. "Nah. Sorry, but you're not my type."

"I'm not?" I look down at my sandals. They've gotten dusty on the walk over here.

"So f-f-ind someone else. Okay?"

"Oh." If I had a white cane with a red tip, I'd close my eyes and tap my way back home.

"It's Yvonne I'm crazy about," he goes. "Tell her. She's the one!"

"Yvonne? *Yvonne?*"

"Yeah, she's a babe. Look, don't cry."

"I'm not crying," I say, but it's a lie. I can feel my tears rolling down my face.

"Sorry," he goes. "You're a cute girl and everything. Really. Hey, why don't you try Slab? Four doors down. He thinks you're hot."

The farther away you get from something, the smaller it seems. But Jimmy's car, as I back away, his face in the window, looks huger and huger. I bump into a tree. It hits my back. But I don't care.

I am still walking backwards when a boy comes out of a house. His name is Henry Weaver. He's a senior, but he's in my English Skills class. "Whoa, Karen, are you okay?"

I don't answer.

His car keys are in his hand like he's a person who goes places, not far, but definitely places. "Need a ride to school, sweetheart?"

"Are you Slab?"

"That's what my buds call me."

"Your buds?"

He opens the door on the passenger side, and I give him points for that, for opening my door, for calling me sweetheart.

"Yeah, my Budweisers." He laughs, but I don't see what's so funny about a beer. "You been crying?"

"Allergies."

"Get in."

I get in. "Why do they call you Slab?"

"Because I'm like cement, man. You'd need a sledgehammer to break me. That's what they used to call my girlfriend, Kathleen. Sledgehammer."

I know the Kathleen he means. She's tough; if she asked you for a cigarette and you said no, she'd probably kick your ass, even if she knew you didn't smoke.

"Is she still your girlfriend?"

"No. I'm free, baby."

"I'm not a baby."

"So I've heard." He pats my leg. It's a friendly pat, I guess, but it makes my stomach go in knots.

Slab's car is not very tidy. There are beer cans, Butterfingers wrappers, cigarette butts and old assignments on the floor. One of them is from English. The teacher has written in large letters, TRY HARDER, HENRY!

Slab's tires seem to shriek as he veers out of the driveway. He takes a sharp left onto Santa Monica Boulevard, then another left at about sixty miles an hour, driving right past our high school.

"Where are you going?"

"It's not every day a beautiful girl steps into my car. Let's take the day off."

"We'll get in trouble."

"I can forge anyone's name on the planet. Don't worry." He massages my knee.

"I have a test in French."

"Why don't I take you for breakfast? I know a place in Topanga Canyon that serves amazing Bloody Marys."

"Isn't that alcohol?"

"The waiter's my cousin. He'll serve us anything we want. His name's Carlo. He is such a trip. He's an actor, only he never really gets a part. And he wrote a screenplay about modern-day cowboys who ride around on Harleys and shoot up Seven-Elevens. Carlo has worked for all these celebrities who've been involved in scandals: Kato Kaelin, the guy who rented a guest house from O. J. Simpson. Remember him?"

"Uh-huh," I say, but what I'm remembering is Yvonne trying to talk me out of liking Jimmy. Because she liked him. To be a witch is to tell the truth; that's the most important thing about a coven. A coven is a covenant, a promise between members. She lied to me and broke the covenant.

"Next Carlo worked for Mel Gibson. Now, that guy is a major jerk. Dumb as a doornail. That's what Carlo says. One time Carlo cleaned Winona Ryder's house. He says, 'Always a celebrity employee, never a celebrity.' You know like 'Always a bridesmaid, never a bride.' Oh yeah, he worked for Donald Trump, for like a day. Trump looks in the mirror five hundred times a day and combs his hair over his bald spot. Trump fired Carlo for tasting his cognac. Expensive stuff. Now Carlo's found Jesus. He wears a cross the size of your hand. But he'll take care of *us*. He's good people. I've done him a lot of favors. You comfortable?"

"Yeah," I say, but I'm anything but comfortable. The one I love can't stand me. My best friend has betrayed me. I started the day wanting to take control of my life. Now here I am: in the passenger seat.

CHRISSIE

Tonight I finally agree to go out with Mom and Max for dinner. I'm in an intensely bad mood because (A) I asked if Yvonne and Karen could come and Mom said no, that we needed "family time." (B) Trish Vandevere had the nerve to ask me for help in biology twice, after she's tormented me for weeks. (C) Jason called while I was out, then wasn't home when I called him. At least Sam was really friendly today in school. He told me he was probably going to go to school back East, maybe even University of Vermont. That made me smile *so* much. His dad grew up in Boston and still thinks New England's the only place to go to college.

We drive in Max's claustrophobic little Porsche to this restaurant in Laurel Canyon called Macro-joy. It's on the side of a cliff and the whole place is outdoors. There is no inside dining. It's sunny La-La Land.

The menu is ridiculous: seaweed broth, seaweed-wrapped tofu, miso paste on fettuccini, bean sprouts and alfalfa juice. I kid you not.

Max is one of these typical Californians who has convinced himself that he is never going to age or die. Seriously, I haven't seen a single cemetery.

Vermont is filled with old graveyards. There are three just on the way to school, peaceful places with old maple trees and birches. Jason and me and some of our friends would hang out there sometimes, leaning against the stones, talking about everything on this planet and beyond.

Am I romanticizing? Was I ever bummed or bored or lonely in Vermont? A couple of times. Maybe. But not much.

The waiter brings us water with no ice. He looks like he's time-traveled from the sixties: hair down to his shoulders and a long beard. He's wearing a T-shirt that says GRATEFUL DEAD. It's cut off so I can see his stomach and his armpits. Gross!

"It was so nice to finally get to talk to Karen and Yvonne last week," Mom says. "I mean, I honestly felt you were trying to hide them from me. I remember being embarrassed by my mom. I thought she was the worst-dressed person on the planet. Well, she was, actually. She wore housedresses. You know? Like these baggy robes."

Max laughs dutifully.

Mom insisted on taking me and my friends out for Indian last weekend and grilling them with questions, her way of being friendly. They were both charmed by her, naturally. Mom could charm an entire country although Yvonne sized her up, too. Later Yvonne said, "I disagree that your mom doesn't care she made you move here. I think she feels really bad. She's just a person who blocks what she feels."

"Yvonne is a little scary, though," Mom says. "Don't you think so, Max?"

"Huh? No. Different. Not scary. Is she Italian?"

"Romanian," I say. Not that I feel like answering. "And German."

"I got the feeling she was looking right into my soul. Isn't that funny?" Mom says.

"She probably was."

"Very nice girls," Max says. "Both of them. We should all go to Disneyland or something."

"Disneyland?" It comes out snide. Mom glares at me.

"Or . . . somewhere else? Universal Studios. San Diego."

The waiter coughs to get our attention, although it's an unhealthy cough.

I order a soy burger and mashed yams, and entertain myself by wondering how fast the deck we're sitting on will slide into the canyon in an earthquake.

"We've finally chosen a place for the reception," Mom says. "Wolfgang Puck's."

"Who's Wolfgang Puck?"

"A chef, silly."

"Oh, I thought it was a hockey implement."

Mom laughs. Her happiness is *disgusting*. "His restaurant is Spago. The food is going to be dazzling. You'll love it, Chrissie."

"I hope they serve lots of casseroles," I say, referring to Dad's funeral, how our friends brought all these meals to freeze, assuming, rightly, that we'd never want to lift a finger again, not to cook, not to do anything. But Mom doesn't get the reference.

"No, silly. Casseroles are so heavy for a spring wedding. Look, here's the menu." She digs in her purse. "Scallops with caper caviar, hazelnut-crusted goat cheese, tilapia ceviche with lemon foam . . ."

"I wish we were eating *there* tonight."

"Well, if you really want to"—Max looks at me brightly—"we can just eat a little here, then see if we can get a table at Spago."

God, he is so eager to please that I could barf. "If this wedding is going to be so great, why can't I invite Yvonne and Karen?"

"At three hundred dollars a head," Mom coos, "I

don't think so. We're not made of money, you know. And we'd have to invite their families. Do you think Yvonne's dad even owns a suit? He looks a little like a terrorist. Don't you think so, Max?"

"Not really," he says, politely.

"Besides, I want you to mingle with your aunt and cousins instead of skulking and judging everyone with your friends."

"My cousins are homicidal maniacs."

"That sounds interesting." Max laughs.

"Clemson accidentally ran over Bensen with Cherry's car last summer," Mom explains. "It could've been tragic."

"I thought they were little kids," Max says.

"They *are*. The twins are just eight, and I'll tell you; that was the last time Cherry ever left the keys in the ignition."

"Was yours and Dad's wedding fancy?" I interrupt.

"Of course not. We were still in college. We had our friends bring food. We bought some wine and had a bonfire in the woods. We wrote our own vows."

"It sounds beautiful."

"It was." Mom yawns. I tend to exhaust her. "But it was also disappointing. I'd always dreamed of something more traditional."

The waiter brings heaping plates. Just as he sets mine down, he sneezes.

"The food's here." Max sounds relieved.

I try not to eat, but eventually my appetite gets the best of me. I decide not to say another word. To punish them, yeah, but also because I feel a little guilty about being rude to Max all the time. I have an overdeveloped conscience, like my dad.

After dinner, they drag me to this New Age bookstore on Melrose (street of weirdos). I sip herb tea while Max picks out yoga DVDs. Then I buy a pack of tarot cards for Yvonne and a crystal for Karen. Despite their wedding budget, Max and Mom are both very free with cash.

When I get home, I call Yvonne to gripe about the lovebirds. She's kind of like a psychotherapist. She listens well and doesn't give advice, just spells, which are abstract enough not to be annoying.

"Chrissie, I've been trying to call you."

"I was out to dinner with Yin and Yang. You wouldn't believe the restaurant. It was so hippie that the waiter's armpits showed. Gross."

"Have you talked to Karen?"

"No. Why wasn't she at school?"

"It's weird. I called her house and her mom said she didn't want to come to the phone. I said, 'Is she barfing or something?' I'm pretty close with her mom, so I can say stuff like that. And she goes, 'No, she just doesn't feel up to talking right now.' She sounded as perplexed as I am."

"Well, maybe she has cramps."

"Karen has never *not* come to the phone. Never. When she had her tonsils out she came to the phone and whistled so I'd know she was there."

"I'm sure it's nothing."

"I have a bad feeling."

"We'll see her in school tomorrow."

"Yeah, I guess. I'd better go in case she calls me back. My dad's too cheap to get call waiting."

"Okay," I say, but I feel hurt. I mean, it tells me where I stand, which is third.

Max and Mom are giggling in the living room, so I head up the invisible stairs to my room and pull out my Writers Workshop application.

Please submit your 3 best poems. I try to write *3 best poems.*

But all I can come up with are a few objects. *Spool of thread,* I write. *Birthday cake.* Then I think of words to go with them: *Unwind. Thud. Splat.*

JIMMY

What is it with those sparrows? There must be a million of them diving like fighter planes toward the lawn. It's like that old Hitchcock movie *The Birds,* where the birds attack people and peck out their eyes.

It is hot, man, about ninety. Hot enough to fry an egg on the sidewalk, my mom used to say. One time when I was little I tried it; cracked the egg and dumped it onto the cement. I watched, but it just quivered there, a would-be chicken, a zero. I was so bummed that nothing happened, that the egg didn't harden itself into something useful like an omelet. And mad at my mom for saying that if it wasn't true.

But hell. Who knows? She's from Texas. Maybe it worked in Texas.

Our plants are all drooping. Isn't that a kick? The great horticulturist can't even water his own plants. I should let them die, show my old man what happens when you neglect things. But I won't. Why should the plants suffer? My mom thinks they have feelings, plants. She used to play music for them, said they grew better. I'll just go around and water them. They perk up fast. Like me when I've had a drink or two.

Happy birthday to me. I'm eighteen years old. Save the balloons for later. Saturday night, and I've called Yvonne three times, checked the machine for a return call at least, even if she just tells me to get lost. *Nada.* Just a message from my mom telling me to have a happy birthday, saying she'll take me to dinner in a week or so. *Or so.* Why couldn't I have been home to answer the phone? My usual luck.

My dad left me a present, a Swiss Army knife, something you'd give to an eight-year-old. At least it's something. I put it in my pocket. The card looks like it's for a kid too, a photo of a grizzly bear in some national park.

Have a nice Birthday, he's written. *Sorry I can't be home. It's growing season.* His excuse for never being home. I mean, when isn't it growing season for something?

The one piece of luck is when I went through his

closet to borrow a clean shirt, I found a bottle of Stoli hidden in the corner of the closet; must have been from Mom's stash. I thought I'd found every bottle she hid.

So this is my party scene. Drink vodka out of a glass—let's get fancy. Just a couple of shots. Study for my biology test, so at least I can graduate.

What's on the menu from Stoner this week? Human genomes. Cloning. Now, there's an idea. Make a duplicate of a perfect specimen. That would be cool. Ten Yvonnes. A row of Yvonnes with dark hair and eyes that go right through your body and into your brain. Eyes that understand what you feel even if you don't know yourself.

Or like me. They could make a me without the gene that craves alcohol, my mom's gene, or a me who never stuttered, never got made fun of, never had to kick anyone's ass to prove myself.

I could call my buds. Go out. Celebrate. But a guy shouldn't have to call people on his own birthday. They should be calling him. I should've gone out with that girl Karen. At least I'd have a girlfriend. I should've never told her to try Slab. I was just trying to make her feel better. Who knew she would actually do it? Another shot. Just to not get too bummed. The way it burns my throat when it goes down, then warms my chest and gut.

There is nothing like that feeling.

Eighteen, and dumb as dirt. So I figure I'll do something right. Monday morning, I'll go to the army recruitment office and enlist. They can send me to Iraq. I'll fight the Muslims. Muslims don't drink, so I'll fight them.

The phone rings. A woman's voice, *Hello,* all sweet and smooth. "Mom?"

Wishful thinking.

"There is a need for blood," the woman says. "There are shortages."

I don't know why, maybe the three shots, but it takes me a second to catch on. "Blood? Who is this?"

"The Red Cross. What is your type?"

"My type? Jerk. Loser. That's my type."

She slams down the phone.

That calls for another shot.

The phone rings.

I pick it up. "Screw you, lady!"

"Okay, but I'd rather celebrate!"

"Slab?"

"My man. Happy birthday."

"You remembered?" I go, sounding like a girl, my eyes stinging.

"Course I remembered. How many of your birthday parties have I been to?"

"Yeah." And he's right. Our moms were buddies all their lives, more even than we were. They'd drink iced tea and rum and smoke and gripe about the bastards they were married to while me and Slab would sit in a kiddy pool and try to drown each other.

"You tying one on?" Slab goes.

"I'm gonna join the army."

"Grim and me and Meth got some Cuervo Gold. We're on our way. We figure we'll walk down to the pier."

"Cool."

"Open the door, dude."

I rush to the door, only I forget to let go of the phone. I pull the damn thing out of the wall, but who the hell cares? Yvonne's never going to call. They're there, all three of them, grinning on the sidewalk, each of them with a bottle in their hands.

"You are the man. You are the man," Grim goes, and Meth gives me a high five. "To the pier, birthday boy. We're gonna fly like birds."

"Wow," I go. "I was just, like, thinking of birds."

"Synchronicity, man," Grim goes. "That is synchronic."

"Gail's doing, like, this Rollerblading exhibition," Meth says.

"You should see the chicks in their bikinis," Slab adds. "I'm gonna get me some tonight."

"To the man," Meth toasts me, opening the Cuervo and passing it to me.

"Cool," I say, 'cause everything's cool. It's my birthday and my buds remember.

I say to them, "I'm gonna join the army," but then

these babes drive by in a convertible, and Slab yells out, "Hey, give us a ride."

They stop and smile at us. There's only two, but they're beautiful. So we run for the car, but as soon we get close they take off, squealing and screaming, leaving us in the dust. "Bitches," Slab yells, and I remember one reason why I don't party with him much. The booze makes him mean. "Someone's gonna pay for that," he says.

"Hey, chill." Grim lights a joint. They try to pass it to me, but I don't want it. I like my poison in liquid form.

We walk toward the beach, and Slab's still grumbling. Twice I say I'm joining the army but no one says anything back, so it's like I'm really not. Meth and Grim start giggling and thinking everything's really funny because of the pot. "Man, that is so cool," Meth goes, pointing to a sign that's flickering.

"Those lights are so spazzed," Grim adds.

"Really," Meth says.

But I just watch the sidewalk move under my feet.

We strut past restaurants and dressed-up people drinking glasses of wine and eating dinner, and I just . . . I just want that life. And I know I won't have it. There's something I'd have to be given to have that life, something I'd need to *do,* and I don't know what it is.

Then we see two kids on skateboards. They're

about nine, and they're laughing. Cute kids. Nothing wrong with them. But as we pass them, Slab reaches out and knocks one of 'em off his board. Grim and Meth are giggling like crazy. But I'm at the point in my drunk where things don't seem so funny. I look back and the kid is sprawled on his back and bawling, and the other kid is hunched over him like a mom, and my stomach twists like before I puke. The streets are tilting. Something is swinging back and forth in my body, like a pendulum on a clock going *no time, no time*. So I yell back at the kids: "Faggots!"

Slab gives me a high five. "Dude! You are the man!"

"The man," the others echo.

Then we turn the corner, and I'm glad 'cause the kids are out of sight, and their faces are just air now, the mom-kid's face looking at me when I said that, clear and harsh, like a judge and jury going *guilty*.

"Man, I'm hungry." Grim grabs his stomach.

"Me too," Meth says.

"Yeah, I'm starved." The tequila and vodka making their way up my throat.

"You got any dough?" Slab asks.

"Nah," we all say. I try to think when I ate last, but all I can remember is school lunch yesterday, something with noodles and ground-up meat.

"Hey, here's an ATM," Meth goes. "Ask and you shall receive."

"Who's got an ATM card?"

"I stole my dad's, but I didn't, like, have the code," Meth says, frowning, "and the machine swallowed it up."

"Know how much money's in there?" Grim says. "And shit, you could practically open that thing with a screwdriver."

"*I* could open that thing with my Swiss Army knife." I pull out my birthday present. "I could open it with the corkscrew."

Slab says, "Well, my man, since you're joining the army, by all means, use your army knife."

So he actually heard me after all.

I pull out my knife and twist out the corkscrew.

"My man. My man," they chant.

"That's not gonna open gotz," Meth goes, which I know, but still, it's my birthday, and I am the man. I dance up to the machine and clown around with the buttons. They laugh and applaud. I stick the corkscrew into the slot where the money comes out. Not for one second do I think it will work, but here's the thing: the corkscrew gets stuck. And it's my present, right, so I'm trying to get it out without breaking it.

Meth and Grim shout something at me. Slab goes, "Shit! Jimmy!" Then I hear footsteps running. And all of a sudden, there's flashing lights, like the other morning outside my house. "Slab?" I go. "Dudes?" But there's just the blue lights, the red, and a couple of cops with their guns drawn, coming toward me like I'm in a movie. And I'm the star, right? I'm the star of the movie because I am the man.

I am the man.

CHRISSIE

Mix together semisweet chocolate, marshmallows,
walnuts, and coconut. Place on graham crackers,
heat in the oven at 350° for five minutes, then eat
for strength. Light a bundle of sage in each room,
staring at the light until you could be anywhere on
the planet, then remember: You are your own
home.

In biology, we're dissecting worms. Yawn!

"Why can't I transfer to chemistry since that's
what I'm interested in?" I begged Stoner before class.

"What's so great about chemistry?"

"It's what I want to be!" As soon as I said it, I knew it was right. Yvonne says it's part of being a witch: having something pop into your head and knowing it's true, like that image of a seagull that keeps coming to me. "My dad was a chemist."

"I'm sure he's a good one." Stoner missed the past tense.

"But I've done this all before," I complained.

He shook his head like it was an alien thing to want to actually learn something rather than slide by. "I told you I asked the guidance counselor. You entered midsemester. Priority goes to seniors and they all put off chemistry until the last semester. You're an anomaly."

So now I'm staring at the worm. Meet the worm. It looks like something that was sneezed onto the table. Stoner is going on about scientific ethics. But I can't concentrate to save my life. I'm worried about Karen, who still hasn't come to school or to the phone for either of us; her mom keeps saying she doesn't feel well. I'm worried that I pissed off Jason last night when I asked him why he doesn't have time for me.

"Earth to Chrissie," Stoner says.

"Huh?"

There are a couple of titters.

Mind occupation. Sometimes it happens when you don't want it to.

"I asked you the scientific name of your friend there."

I peer down at the corpse. *"Ascaris lumbricoides."*

"Wow." Sam gives me a high five.

"Very good. We like to think of smaller life-forms as beneath us, when in reality . . ." The door to the classroom opens and Trish limps in. "You're late."

"The heel broke on my shoe." She holds up a leg to show him, then she plops down at her lab table: "What is that thing?"

"That, Ms. Vandevere, is an *Ascaris lumbricoides,* and you are going to dissect it."

"I thought that was next week. I was planning to be absent," Trish says. "Gross."

"May I point out that you will be doing to this worm what your father does to people's faces?"

"What does her dad do?" I whisper to Sam.

"Plastic surgeon."

"Very funny," Trish says. "Weren't there kids who protested or something and went to court so they wouldn't have to do this?"

"That was a frog, not a worm, and they protested before the fact, not on the day of. Just look at the PowerPoint diagram if you're in doubt."

I dissect mine in about two seconds and fill in the report. Then I entertain myself by peeking at Sam's drawing of a worm with Trish Vandevere's head.

Trish has her arms folded and she's talking to the

girl who sits next to her. When Trish's lab partner is done with his, he tugs her worm over and dissects it. Stoner doesn't say a word. It's so annoying.

"Have you been to Venice Beach yet?" Sam whispers to me.

"Not yet. I heard it's cool. My mom is so busy, it's hard to get a ride anywhere. I can't wait to turn sixteen and get a car."

"No kidding. You're nothing without a car in So. Cal. Once I can drive, I'm heading north every weekend. Santa Barbara, San Luis Obispo. That's where California gets nice."

"Really?" I say. *Take me with you.*

"It's a completely different state."

"That, I'd like to see." I feel myself blush, because it kind of sounds like I'm inviting myself.

"And you've got to see San Francisco and Big Sur."

The bell rings. We gather our things. I want to follow him and keep talking, but I have a habit of waiting for Trish to clear out first, in case she decides to bug me (no offense to the worm).

When I finally come out, Trish is still in the hall, chugging from a bottle of Evian and going on about how mean Stoner is. All the kids with their two-dollar bottles of water don't consider the fact that over a billion people in the world do not have safe drinking water and the number is growing. Or that every ten seconds, a child dies from a water-related disease. Or that my dad spent his life trying to remedy it.

"Oh, look." She points her bottle at me. "It's the Wicked Witch of the East. You'd better watch out or someone will drop a house on you."

I'd love to knock her off her one high heel; I truly don't *get* people who like to attack others for no reason. Instead, I hiss the spell to turn her into what she is: "Getama, Salona, Reptiva, Toad!"

She jumps back like I hit her. "What did you just say?"

"I think she put a spell on you." A jock grins at me.

"Oh, I am *so* scared," Trish whines, but it's weird. She really does look scared.

YVONNE

Chop onions until you cry. Chant the prayer for de-
tachment. Run around the block seventeen times
until you can't move. Eat chocolate until all you
feel is the race of the sugar in your blood, and
pain is obliterated like your past.

There are many theories about the origin of witches.
Most say witchcraft evolved out of pagan rituals,
which have existed since time began. The word *witch*
means to twist or bend, as in bending fate, or twisting
reality. It also means wisdom. Witchcraft was accepted
until the fourteenth century, when witches were

accused of worshipping the devil. They were persecuted, tortured and jailed. Everyone knows about the Salem witch trials in this country during the 1600s. Teenage girls accused people of witchcraft. Those accused were hanged, stoned or drowned. Mostly, those accused of being witches were women.

The only thing more misunderstood than a witch is a Gypsy. The Gypsies came to Germany in 1417. Before that there's no record of them. It's as if they appeared from thin air. The Gypsies told the Germans that they were from Little Egypt. But no one was sure where that was. Like witches, they were initially accepted. But then they, too, were persecuted. In World War II they were put into concentration camps along with the Jews.

To be a Gypsy is to know you'll get unwanted attention. To be a Gypsy is to express yourself anyway.

To be a witch is to own your power as a girl: intuition, emotion, intelligence, depth. Nowadays, it's no big deal, just another harmless fad like yoga or feng shui.

What am I talking about? Nothing helps. Being a witch is pretending you have control over a universe that is more random and chaotic than a loose tornado. Being a witch is playing make-believe because life is boring, disorderly, unjust . . .

It's just a game.

It's nothing.

Karen came to my house and ended our friendship,

the only friendship I've ever had, aside from my dad and Chrissie. Gina Sorino drove up in front of my house and Karen jumped out of the car. She dumped ten years' worth of gifts on the lawn: a feather boa I gave her in third grade, the shell necklace I made last summer, my Ouija board, the silk blouse we chipped in on at the vintage shop in Hollywood and took turns wearing, my yellow bikini, a heart-shaped box of candy I gave her on Valentine's Day.

"You stole Jimmy," she shouted. "You cast a spell on him."

For the first time in my life, the black cat got *my* tongue. My mouth opened and nothing came out. I couldn't say a word in my defense.

"Thief!" she shrieked, and then she threw up, right on the dead grass in front the sidewalk. I had the creepiest feeling that she was throwing up *me*.

Gina Sorino was watching all this from her car. After Karen dumped her stuff and jumped back into Gina's car, Gina gave me a little wave, like *Hello/goodbye*. Very cheerful. Not like *I have just witnessed you having your heart ripped out and have stolen your best friend*. And that, too, left me stunned. The sheer lack of meanness or gloating. There is nothing in Gina's brain. Maybe a lawn chair or a potted plant. That's it.

Is this always going to happen to me? People disappearing?

Every time the phone rings, I think it's Karen. If it's a telemarketer, I'm so angry I don't even say "No, thank you," I just slam down the phone. This time, it's Chrissie. Thank God there's Chrissie. She's going on about Sam Levy, how she ran into him at Java the Hut and he bought her a smoothie. Her words are Ping-Pong balls bouncing around. She's only known Karen a few months; what's it to her?

"Do you think he likes me?" she asks.

"Uh-huh." My voice cracks.

"What's wrong?"

I tell her the story, holding my breath between sentences so I won't cry.

"That's why Karen wasn't returning our calls? Jimmy? That creepy boy? I can't believe it."

"Neither can I," I whisper.

"Give her a few days to calm down. Instant-message her and tell her nothing happened. Or send her a letter, even."

As hard as she tries, Chrissie will never be a witch. Her first impulse is always logic. "Karen has never been mad at me. Ever."

"I'll go to her house and talk to her."

"Nothing is going to help." I blink back tears. "She gets crazy about boys."

There is a knock on the door, but I don't answer it. It's always some tenant whining about a leaking faucet or running toilet. The knocking grows into pounding. "Dad!" I call. "Someone's at the door."

He doesn't answer me.

"Hang on, Chrissie. I'd better get the door." Even though the phone is a portable, I set it down.

A woman is there. She wears jeans, a USC T-shirt, and Birkenstocks. She has long black hair. It's hard to tell how old she is. Forty? Fifty?

"What apartment do you live in? I'll tell my dad to come check out the problem."

My dad comes up behind me. He's in his pajamas, battleships sailing across them—his kid pajamas, I call them. "Did you ask who it was before you opened the door?" He's very friendly to the tenants, so I'm shocked when he lunges forward and tries to slam the door shut, even more surprised when she shoves the door back. They struggle until she wedges her body in the opening and slides inside like a snake.

Here's the thing. My dad has never, ever been violent. He swerves his car to avoid a raccoon or a cat. He can't stand to watch police shows or action movies, except *Star Wars*. The customer is always right, no matter how rude.

But now he shoves her against the wall and shouts at her in German. I grab the phone to call the police, and there's Chrissie's voice. "Yvonne. My God. What's happening?" And only when I say it into the phone do I know. "My mom is here," I say. Then everything goes black.

I wake up and feel two parents, one on either side of me, my dad holding my wrist. *Her* hand on my forehead. Wizard is sitting, purring, on my chest. I keep my eyes closed.

"She's breathing," she says in accented English.

"She must have fainted. Vonny."

"That is not her name."

"Her name is none of your business."

"You stole her from me. Left an imprint of a child on my sheets that has never gone away."

"You're full of it. You know that? You have always been full of it! That cat is a better mother than you."

"I need a cigarette." She lets go of me.

"Yes, it's always what *you* need."

I hear the flick of a lighter, the inhaling of smoke.

"No smoking in my house," my dad says.

"Ciella's never liked to see violence. Remember when Caucus knifed Rom and he fell into the river? She ran into the woods and it took me hours to find her."

"Me."

"Huh?"

"*I* found her," my dad says.

"You did not. It was me."

"No, it was me! And if you'll recall, it was Rom who knifed Caucus, and it was over *you*. You brought misery to any man who got involved with you."

"Oh, shut up."

"You can't argue with that, can you?"

"She's beautiful."

"Yes."

"She looks like me."

"But she's not *like* you. Fortunately."

"She's back. She's awake and listening."

How does she know?

The phone is ringing. Dad gets up. I hear him answer. *She* blows cigarette smoke in my face. I practically choke. But I keep still. My dad says, "It's okay. I'll have her call you later, Chrissie. Bye, hon."

"You can stop playing dead now," she says dryly.

It's weird. My whole life I've waited for her to come back, and now she's here and it's nothing like I imagined. Her voice is brittle. And I feel angry at her, protective of my dad, even though he's the one who took me from her.

"How did you find us?" he asks.

"By the surface of the clouds, by birds circling your roof . . ."

"Oh, cut the crap, Morgana. I'm not one of your idiot followers."

She shrugs. "The Internet. You should've changed your name if you didn't want to be found."

"Leave her. Leave us. We're happy. You were a terrible mother."

"Maybe so," she admits, "but I've changed."

"How did you get to America?"

"A man."

"Of course. There's always a man." His voice is bitter. "Where is he? Outside? Waiting to steal her back?"

"He's dead. He brought me here. Three years ago. He was a nice man."

"Did you kill him?"

"Ha! I have never killed anyone. It's you who killed me. Who stole the only thing I ever cared about."

"Yvonne is not a thing!"

"Her name is not Yvonne."

"Now it is, and you'd better remember that! So how did he die? This man."

"Old age. That's how. His heart went out."

"You ran around with some old man?"

"You wonder why our marriage went sour. This is it. You have no respect!" She goes into the kitchen. "What have you got to eat?"

"Nothing." He shakes my shoulder. "Yvonne, wake up."

"She's faking. Throw some cold water on her."

"Shut up, Morgana."

I open my eyes and sit up. My dad helps me stand.

"I'm going to make soup," she says. "Where's the onions?"

"Yvonne hates soup. We both hate soup. Soup is too hot for California."

"I'll make cold soup." She waves a wooden spoon, then points it at me. "*You* wished me here. *You* pulled me here like a magnet. I could feel it."

"You said it was the Internet!" my dad shouts.

"Same thing."

Her hair is threaded with gray and much coarser than mine. Her eyes are dark and big. But her expression is not like what I imagined. Her face is hard. Her eyes dart around like she's looking for something to steal. The gut feeling I get is not great.

"I haven't eaten all day," she says.

"You think you're moving in here?" Dad asks.

"No. I'm staying at Motel Six. Set the table, Ciel . . . Yvonne." A point for my dad.

But I don't move.

"Get out of my kitchen." Dad sounds tired. "Out of my life."

She sets the spoon down. What if she *does* walk out and disappears again? But then she turns and opens the refrigerator. She pulls out an onion and tomatoes.

"Put the vegetables down," Dad says.

I suppress a giggle. It just sounds so nutty.

"You." She turns to me. "Have you heard of Ignaz Semmelweis?"

I don't answer.

"In the eighteen hundreds, in Austria, Dr. Semmelweis proved the connection between mothers dying in childbirth and the lack of hand washing by doctors. From the Vienna toilet cleaners, he got the idea that doctors should wash their hands with chloride of lime between medical procedures, so they didn't infect the mothers. Do you know what happened to him for making such a truthful and amazing discovery?"

Why is she telling me this? I shrug.

"I'll tell you. Semmelweis was fired from his job, harassed by his colleagues and driven out of the country. He died in an asylum from the same infection that hundreds of thousands of mothers died from because no one listened to his advice. So much for truth. So much for faith in the system."

"What the hell is this about?" Dad demands.

"Among illegal immigrants in this great country, the infant and maternal mortality rates are almost that of nineteenth-century Vienna."

"So?" Dad says.

"So . . . I'm working in the camps for illegal immigrants, up and down the coast. I'm the midwife. I want Ciella to come live with me. It's my turn to have her now."

CHRISSIE

SPELL TO DISAPPEAR

One mauve taffeta dress two sizes too small, brown mousy hair, glasses, a figure like a lumpy tube of toothpaste. Put the object in a room with beautiful people, blond and tanned, and snap . . . she's nobody.

I wrote my own spell to describe the feeling of being here, at Mom's wedding reception, with a roomful of strangers, give or take a relative or two. The whole wedding has been so perfect, from the flowers—lilies and birds of paradise—to the food. And Mom looks perfect; that's the worst thing about her.

If Yvonne and Karen had been here this could have been fun. But they wouldn't come together anyway. Everything's changed.

I hate change. That's the root of the problem.

Max is now my stepdad. Yvonne's mom shows up and wants to drag her away for the summer. Karen's not speaking to Yvonne, so by default she barely speaks to me. It stinks. Two friends reduced to one. And over what? A stupid boy. I can't stand it.

So what could be worse? This! I'm heading to the champagne fountain, and my worst enemy appears in a bright red cocktail dress. My friends aren't invited, but Trish Vandevere is. That says it all.

I want to turn around and make a beeline for the fancy bathroom with the stuffed chairs (I've already spent an hour or so there), but she sees me. Besides, this is *my* mom's wedding, after all. Why should I have to run and hide?

"Chrissie!" she exclaims (the first time she has ever used my name). "What are *you* doing here?"

"What am I doing here?"

"This is the last place I'd expect to run into *you*."

"It's my mom's wedding!" I say. *Duh!* "It's usually good form to go to your own mom's wedding."

"Ava is your mother? Are you, like, adopted?"

Great! "I don't remember *your* name on the guest list." *Not that I ever saw one.*

"My dad is friends with Max. And since my dad's between wives, I get to be his date. It's killer boring."

131

"Thanks."

"You know what I mean. There's no one our age or even close. It's just . . . I get tired of being the sub. As soon as my dad gets a girlfriend, he'll drop me like a hot potato."

I know the feeling. After Dad died, Mom couldn't stand sleeping in her room alone, so we each took a couch and watched old movies or the cooking channel until we fell asleep. Usually, I would go to Jason's and help him with his farm chores, but she wanted me to be home all the time, so he started coming over a lot more.

But then the business trips started—always to L.A. She stopped needing me. I didn't know why, then.

"Listen, I want to ask you something," Trish says.

"What?"

"That day when you said all those crazy words to me, were you really casting a spell?"

"Why does it matter?"

"It's just that all these bad things keep happening. My boyfriend dumped me. I got this gross case of acne. We had a fire in our kitchen and our house is unlivable. The insurance company put us up in the *Comfort Inn*. They have these "continental" breakfasts, but they don't say from what continent. Like . . . *Canada*?"

"Canada is not a continent."

"Look, I know I haven't been that pleasant to you. I have this way of taking my frustrations out on others. That's what my therapist said. It's just . . . if you put a spell on me, I don't need it. I've had a hard enough time."

"It was just a joke."

"Really?"

"Totally."

"Well, even if was a joke, can you . . . take away the spell?"

"Sure, as long as you leave me alone at school."

"Okay. I'll leave you alone."

"Karen and Yvonne, too."

"Fine. I won't bug any of you."

I can't wait to tell Yvonne! What power!

To celebrate, I go to the champagne fountain, and fill my glass, and say a toast to my witches. It's the first alcohol I can remember having, and it's not bad, like 7-Up. Then I fill my plate and join my "side of the family," which consists of Mom's sister, Cherry, and her twin boys, Clemson and Bensen, who are under the table shoving deserts into their mouths.

"Hi, Aunt Cherry." I plop down next to her.

"Did your mom say you could drink?"

"Max did." I lie, although if I asked him, I know he'd say yes. "How come Uncle Shep didn't come?"

"Work. Always work. Isn't it a coincidence that as soon as I had twins, he got a job where he's on the road all the time, and never to good places like France or the Bahamas? He goes to Detroit and Huntsville and Dallas."

"Can I get you anything?"

"I've had plenty. The food is fabulous. I've never seen so many glamorous people in one place, and that singer sounds like Frank Sinatra. It's a hoot."

"Yeah. They know how to do things up."

"What do you think of Max?"

"He's okay."

"He's never been married before, your mom said. Isn't that strange? At his age? But no kids, lucky for you. Imagine if you were saddled with a bunch of stepsiblings."

"Yeah, I guess that is lucky."

"Your mom says you're going to a poetry camp in Vermont."

"I applied."

"I thought science was your thing."

"It is, but I also write poems. It's supposed to be pretty hard to get in. Mostly, I just wanted to get back to Vermont."

"You'll get in. You're all brains, one hundred percent, your dad's daughter all the way."

Usually, I would consider that a compliment, but I have a feeling it's also her way of saying I'm not pretty. "Thanks."

"Do you have a boyfriend yet?"

"The boy I like lives in Vermont."

"That just won't do, Chrissie. You need to get a life here. Look at your mom. She's in her element."

"I'm trying not to look at my mom, in general."

"Don't be so hard on her." Cherry frowns. "She's happy. Don't you want her to be happy?"

"Not if it means I don't get to be."

"She didn't belong in Vermont. You and your dad did, but Ava and I . . . we need warmth and people. We're Southern girls. Look at me in Florida . . ."

"Yeah, and you've both transformed into blondes."

"I know. I love it! Our hair was the same dishwater brown as yours, did you know that? And her highlights! You know who Ava looks like?"

"Meg Ryan."

"Exactly. Ava's pushing forty and she looks younger than you."

"Remind me to look you up when I need a shot of self-esteem," I snap.

"Oh, you know what I mean. You look fine. I think you're losing weight. I know! I'll give you highlights! I went to beauty college for three years."

"College?"

"Well, that's what they called it. But I haven't used it. I'm making more money on Tupperware than I did cutting hair."

"Those plastic containers?"

"Yep. You know, your mom and I, we grew up poor, without prospects, and we made a vow to better ourselves. It wasn't like it is today for you girls, where you are born, literally born, thinking the sky is the limit. When Brownie Wise, who invented the home party for Tupperware, trained women to sell the stuff, she had to ask their *husbands* for permission. She told them, 'You make the bread, let the wife make a little cake.' Can you believe it? Times have changed."

"Bloood!" Clemson shouts, smashing a strawberry into his brother's face.

"Boys!" Cherry yells. "Go play where no one knows you're mine."

"I think I need more champagne." I stand.

"What would your mom say? I'm supposed to be your babysitter."

"She'd say, 'Have fun.' "

"Okay, but make it quick, hon. I've got to get the twins to bed by eight o'clock or they'll turn into monsters."

They already are, I want to tell her.

I don't make it quick. I stand by the champagne fountain, drink another glass, then another. I watch my mom dance with Max and wonder what it would be like to have Jason hold me like that, looking like he'd won the lottery. Or maybe even Sam.

I try to bring to mind times I saw my dad hugging her like that, but I can't. Whenever I remember my dad, he's with me, and we're tapping maples, or snowshoeing, or reading, or searching the woods for Wilbur, and my mom's bundled up by the fire or at her drafting table or watching us out the window.

By the time I return to Aunt Cherry, she's standing with her purse. "I thought someone kidnapped you." Clemson and Bensen are sitting back to back in chairs.

Each has a white cloth napkin stuffed in his mouth. "Don't they look cute like that?"

"Yeah. Perfect."

At home, I warn the kids not to fall off the stairs, then I go to my room, where I find my rejection letter from the Vermont Writers Workshop thrown on my bed.

I toss it in the trash, unopened.

I've drunk enough champagne to fall into an immediate sleep, but I don't sleep well. I'm hot and I keep having the same stupid dream, that Mom and Max beg me to go on their honeymoon with them. Then I dream about Karen, that I'm rubbing the crystal I bought for her and casting a spell to bring her back to us, to the coven, to our friendship. I wake up at 4 a.m., the same time Jason will be getting up in Vermont, where it's seven o'clock.

I'm dying of thirst and I have a headache, so I run downstairs and drink a bottle of Gatorade. Bensen and Clemson are asleep on the floor in front of the TV, looking like angels. Cherry is on the couch, snoring.

I tiptoe up to my room, retrieve the letter from the trash, and open it. *We are delighted,* it says, *to offer you a place at our annual teen poets' conference.*

KAREN

Close your eyes. What do you see behind the shades of your lids? If you see purple spots, passion is driving your sight; if you see white squares, the spirit has entered; if you see red, you are blinded by anger; if you see green, your vision is distorted by false pride. Blue is spirit. Black is black. To restore vision, buy Visine. Put two drops in both eyes (and eat a Hershey's Kiss while you're at it). Then blink three times. Recite the following incantation: "Vision be true. Vision be wise. Show me the real behind the guise."

The eye has many parts to it: the retina, the optic nerve, the iris, the pupil, and the cornea. The socket of bone that holds the eye is called an orbit. The planet of the eye moves in its orbit, a galaxy, the Milky Way. Tears are produced in the lacrimal glands. What are tears, then? Falling stars.

I have made a model of the eye out of Styrofoam and put little flags on toothpicks to label it. This is the kind of useless stuff you have to do in school. The main part of the eye is the vitreous humor, but I don't think there's anything funny about it. I have learned everything there is to know and worked days on my report and model, even though I have no intention of going back to school. Ever.

There are many diseases of vision, from the mild to the severe. The mild might be conjunctivitis. The more severe include glaucoma, gyrate atrophy, corneal edema.

Then there are optical illusions, seeing things that aren't really there, like friendship and loyalty. Or not seeing what *is* there, like betrayal.

Slab took me to this restaurant where his cousin worked. He ordered for me: a double Bloody Mary and a cheese omelet. There's this cartoon I used to watch where a girl is tied to railroad tracks. That's what I wished. That someone would tie me to the railroad tracks and a train would speed over me and wipe away every thought in my head, every feeling.

The Bloody Mary kind of did that. After a while, my fingertips went numb. Then my brain. Slab said nice things to me. He told me I was pretty, and that I should have loads of boyfriends. He said he liked my dress. And he talked nonstop about all kinds of things, mostly rap bands I'd never heard of. Still, I started having a smidgen of fun with him.

After breakfast, he took me to a closed-down gas station his dad used to own. "Have you ever done anything like this? Ducked out of school the whole day and been totally free?"

"No."

"Isn't it an awesome feeling? Freedom. Man, I can't stand being trapped at school."

The place smelled like gasoline and motor oil. I wondered if freedom usually smelled like that. When he lit a candle, I expected the room to explode.

He had a small fridge there with beer, an old tape deck and a sleeping bag. He carried the candle over and got a couple of beers. He said it was his hangout, like a kid might have a fort in the woods. It reminded me of a movie set, but for a bad movie.

There was no electricity, no light aside from the candle. I could barely see. I kept imagining I saw Yvonne out of the corner of my eye, but when I turned my head, she wasn't there. I wished she was.

Slab asked me if he could kiss me, which seemed polite, so I let him. He was a good kisser. Gentle. I pretended it was Jimmy and that everything had gone right, that we were on a nice date and I was going to have a boyfriend.

Then we drank beer and I told him about liking Jimmy. My voice came out funny, like I had a mouthful of gum. He said Jimmy wasn't worth my trouble. Jimmy was a boat without a rudder. Someday he'd just sink. Then he asked, "How 'bout me? Do you like me?"

"I guess." I didn't know what to say. I was like that empty gas station, absorbed by darkness.

"Come closer." Slab pulled me onto his lap. He kissed me, but I didn't feel anything. That's not how it's supposed to be. "You're pretty. And sexy."

He was moving all over the place, then, saying that kind of stuff until none of it meant anything. I wanted to get out of there in the worst possible way, but I didn't say so. I was the passenger.

The candle went out. You would've never known it was light outside. Absorbed by darkness and alcohol, I couldn't tell my hair from his, my limbs from his, or even who I was.

Afterward, I felt sick and didn't want to go to school. I told Slab to drop me on Colorado Avenue, then I ran home. I knew Mom wouldn't be there. She had her embroidery group at the fabric shop. Dad was at work. Only Troy was there, painting the front door.

"Hi! Wanna help?"

"No."

"You hungry? I just went to Zorba the Greek and got a couple of pita pockets. Want to have lunch?"

"Don't you ever go to classes?"

"Not on Tuesdays, so I thought I'd get some work done." He is the most sickeningly cheerful person I know.

"You're gonna flunk."

He frowned. "Are you okay? Why are you home from school? Are you sick?"

I felt like I was going to cry. "No. Maybe."

"Do you need anything? I can run to the store."

I shook my head and ran inside.

I pulled down the shades. I drank all the water I could stand and took off my clothes. If there had been a fire in the fireplace, I would have burned them. But it's not my clothes' fault, it's mine.

I stood in the shower and soaped up my body over and over. I stayed there until there was no more hot water.

Still, I could smell vodka, beer, cigarettes, oil and gasoline, the stench of Slab floating off my skin and hair.

The next morning, when I got to school, the first person I saw was Slab. He was with that girl, Kathleen; he had his arm around her. It made my stomach turn. He had acted like he was going to be my boyfriend.

I went in the side door to avoid him. And there was Jimmy in the hall with his friend, Meth, who's always given me the creeps. It was like all the people I didn't want to see were in my face. Like a nightmare.

When I walked past Meth, he made a gesture at me that made me know Slab had told him. Maybe he told the whole school. Jimmy looked at the floor. At least he didn't join in.

I turned around and ran down the stairs onto the street, all the way to my house. I told my mom I threw up, and she called the school.

Since then, I haven't gone back. I said I was still sick to my stomach, which is true. The nausea started immediately, like a top spinning in my belly, and the dizziness.

"What if you're pregnant?" Gina Sorino asks when I tell her, like the thought hasn't occurred to me. She's my friend, now that Yvonne is not. "I got pregnant once," she says, "and my brother told me that if I rode on a roller coaster the baby would fall out."

"What did you do?"

"I went to a clinic and got rid of it. It was horrible. Then I had to have an AIDS test and be checked for other things. You probably should do that too. Since then, I carry condoms in my purse, just in case, not that there's anybody . . . you should do that. Carry condoms. Do you want me to come get you?"

"Okay."

We drive into Westwood, and past UCLA, where Troy goes to college when he's not loafing at my house.

Then she drives past the clinic where she went. A group of angry people stand at the front carrying signs with pictures of fetuses like peanut shells discarded into a pile. The signs say, WHOSE CHOICE? and MURDER IS A SIN. "Were they there when you had to go?" I ask Gina.

"Uh-huh." She blinks.

There are two ladies from my church there. As we get closer, I cover my face.

"You'd better get a pregnancy test," Gina says. "Then you'll know for sure."

"Isn't it too early? It's only been a couple of days."

"The new ones work right away."

We go to a drugstore. Gina buys the test for me. There's no bathroom so we drive down to the beach and I go in the public one. There's sand on the floor and the door doesn't have a lock, so Gina has to hold it. My hands are shaking so much I almost drop the stick in the toilet.

"Is there a blue line?" Gina asks.

"Not yet."

"Give it five more minutes."

I feel like I'm going to throw up. "Do you have a watch?"

"I'll use my cell phone."

"Are these dependable?"

"Yeah. It said you can tell on the first day."

A woman with tan feet and pink toenails comes into the next stall. She hums "The Star-Spangled

Banner" while she pees. Outside, I hear the Jesus guy singing "Amazing Grace." It's like everyone has some moral lesson for me. "Has it been five minutes?"

"Just about."

"There's no blue line."

"That's good!" Gina says. "Now you don't have to worry."

"Not about that, at least. But I still feel sick."

"Maybe Slab just grossed you out. I think he's gross."

I don't answer, because I know who grosses me out: me. I shove the test back in the box, then come out and throw it in the trash, covering it with paper towels.

"What do you want to do? Now that everything's okay, we can have some fun." Gina is sweet, but I can't have fun with her. I can only have fun with Yvonne, my enemy. Maybe Chrissie.

"I just want to walk on the beach or something."

"Okay."

"I mean . . . I just want to be alone. I'm sorry."

"How will you get home?"

"I'll walk. Or I'll call my mom. Don't worry. You've been really nice. Thanks."

But Gina does look worried. "I don't want to just leave you here."

"It's okay."

"Well, call me if you need a ride."

"I will. I've got my cell. Thanks for being my friend."

★ ★ ★

I walk down to the beach and watch the water. Yvonne always says that the ocean is the place to go when you want your thoughts to be clear. But mine are muddy and confused. I think about losing my best friend, the boy I loved and the little bit of respect I'd earned back for myself. I think about Yvonne's face when I returned all her things.

The tide is low, so I take off my shoes and wade out. The water is cold and the only ones out are surfers in their wet suits. Still, if I swim fast enough, I'll get warm and the water will hold me. A small fishing boat is past the pier. I wonder if I could reach it. I've swum out that far before.

I immerse my whole body like a baptism, then dive under the waves and swim out: beyond the beach and the people on the shore, beyond the waves, beyond Santa Monica and the kids who've made fun of me, beyond Slab and Meth, beyond my shame, beyond Yvonne's betrayal. My limbs are seaweed. My mind is salt water. I swim out like a mermaid, beyond and beyond and beyond.

CHRISSIE

Once upon a time, in Tibet, there was a poor old woman who had a beautiful daughter. As she had no dowry for her daughter, she feared that the girl would not marry and would never escape poverty. One day, a poor man learned of the girl and pretended to be rich in order to marry her. After the wedding, he locked her in a trunk, went to the shack that was his home and put locks on the doors, so that when she found out how poor he was, she wouldn't be able to run away. But a wealthy man found the trunk and broke it open. He was so moved by the girl that he carried her away and married her himself. In her place he locked a bear, so that when the man came back, he was eaten.

That was one of the many tales Dad brought home from the places he traveled: Tibet, India, Nepal, Pakistan, Vietnam. I remember that one, because I always felt sorry for the poor man. I wished he had taken the girl home and she had learned to love him for himself. Together they would make a life as equals.

My dad felt the same way. He wanted the man to get the girl, even if he was deceptive, because he had loved her even though she was poor. Plus, Dad didn't like to think about anyone being eaten by a bear.

Dad said that the best things about his travels were the people and their stories. He met a man in India who had leprosy. The man had lost his fingers, but he laughed and joked with Dad. Dad met families who lived in mud huts, but the kids played like any other kids. His work taught him that there's no relationship between money and happiness, he told me. I can attest to that. From what I can tell, we've got loads of money now. Mom even said I'm getting a new car for my birthday. I can just decide what kind I want, "within limits." The money drawer that used to be filled with dollars now has twenties and fifties. Max probably fills it up.

Last night, Mom made me make a list of things I like about California. She was that annoyed at my griping. She said until I made a list of ten things, I would be grounded. Max shook his head like he thought she was crazy, but he didn't argue on my behalf like he usually does. I guess he's sick of my whining too.

People were not allowed on the list, just things that related to California, so my two witches weren't allowed, or Sam.

Most of my list was food related. First was Java the Hut, which has the best mocha lattes I've ever tasted. Then Jane's Juice, where they make smoothies with fresh fruit, yogurt, bee pollen and protein powder. Next was Cathy's Concoctions, a bakery on Sepulveda that bakes awesome cookies. After that came Thai Juan, then India Mahal, next the Santa Monica Farmers' Market, where you can get fig tamales, organic green chili omelets, and samples of meditation tonic, dried cherries, salsas; the list goes on and on. It's an eating frenzy.

The only place on my list that wasn't food related is Sanctuary. It was Max's idea that I go there for a teen yoga class. I pictured model-thin Santa Monica girls in their unclothes, contorting like pretzels. But Sanctuary is really different. It's like stepping into Japan. You sit on tatami mats at low tables, drink green tea, then go to a ninety minute class of yoga and meditation. It's a silent space. Only the sensei, the teacher, says a few words at the beginning of each class. I can't believe the amount of pressure that relieves, to not speak.

The kids who go there are the kind who "go to the beat of their own drummer," as Mom would say, although she doesn't usually mean it as a compliment. Since I started doing yoga twice a week, I've lost ten pounds without trying and I'm sleeping at night. I feel happier. It's magic.

And I'm less afraid of the waves pounding onto the sand in front of me. I'm waiting for Yvonne, who is late. She left an urgent message on my cell: *Meet me under the pier for a powwow.* As soon as I think of her, she appears.

"Chrissie! Sorry I'm late. I hate being late." She plops down next to me. She's wearing torn jeans, a red velvet jacket and a floppy hat.

"It's cool. How are you?"

"Don't ask."

"Now I have to ask."

"For one thing, there's my so-called mom. She's *hounding* me to go off with her to some immigrant camp this summer, like it's something I owe her."

"No way will your dad let you go."

"True. It's just . . . it's so confusing. She came over again last night. She was wearing the same clothes. What if they're the only clothes she has? And I felt guilty. Ugh," she growls. "Nothing is ever clear-cut. Is it? I mean people. I don't like her. But there's something there that tugs at me."

"Blood?"

She dips her hand in the water. "Blood is like this tide. The moon pulls the heart."

"Remind me to use that in a poem."

"Use that in a poem. How was the wedding?"

"Awful, except one thing." I tell her about Trish.

"Your spell worked. It was amazing. She actually seemed nicer. And she promised not to bug us."

"Spells don't do anything." Yvonne frowns. "It was just a game."

"How can you say that?"

"Because I know."

"They do work. I got into the teen writers' workshop."

"You did? That's *awesome*. You're going to be famous."

"Because of your spell."

"Because of your poems."

"And what about your mom coming back? We did a ton of spells for that."

She smiles. "I didn't think you believed in witchcraft. I thought you just went along to be nice."

"I didn't believe . . . I don't, but maybe magic does happen . . . sometimes."

"Not the magic *I* need."

"Karen will get over it. She has to. You didn't do anything wrong!"

"Have you ever heard of phantom pain? When a limb is severed, the person can still feel it aching. That's how I feel without Karen. I don't even care about my mom, compared to Karen."

I think of Jason, how I spent every day of my life from the age of four with him and now he doesn't have time to call me. "Yeah, I know what you mean."

"I only talked to Jimmy that one time, and I didn't

return his other calls. I was trying to get them to-gether, trying to help. Although I have to admit . . . I *could've* liked Jimmy if Karen didn't like him."

"I don't get why *anyone* likes Jimmy," I blurt.

"I know he seems rough, but he's like a treasure box buried under a shipwreck. There's good stuff in him. I know it."

"If . . ."

"Yeah. A lot of ifs." She throws a handful of sand into the water.

I want so badly to cheer her up. "Guess what?"

"What?"

"I found my animal familiar. I thought it would be something like an elephant or bear, but the image I keep getting is a seagull."

"Really?" Her eyes immediately go to the sky, where a lone gull floats on air currents.

"Yeah."

"A seagull. I'm surprised that's your animal familiar."

"Me too. A scavenger that hangs out at the beach."

"But also freedom and independence." Her face looks sad again. "So you're going off to Vermont for the summer. That'll be great for you."

"I'm not sure. I haven't sent in the deposit yet. I mean, I thought I'd be happier about it."

"Funny how we get things we want and then we're not sure we want them."

"Yeah. It's in Montpelier. That's pretty far from

where I used to live. So it'll be like being a new kid again. I don't know. Every time I look at that acceptance letter, my stomach goes in knots."

"Go with your gut." She finally smiles. "Being a witch is trusting your intuition. I remember one time . . ." Yvonne stops and points to an ambulance racing across the sand toward the shore. "They're pulling someone out of the water."

A police car follows the ambulance, then the lifeguard's truck. Two surfers, seal-like in wet suits, emerge from the waves dragging a body.

"Oh no." I shudder.

"It's a girl." Yvonne jumps up and bolts across the beach. I follow, first slowly, then faster. Because I see what she sees: the white shorts and shoulder-length hair. *Karen.*

"It was weird, man," a surfer is telling the policeman. "She was way out past the pier, like she was trying to swim to England or something."

Yvonne shoves through the crowd and I follow. A cop grabs my shoulder. "She's my friend!" I shout, then I rush forward and kneel next to Yvonne, who is holding Karen's hair out of her face as Karen vomits over the side of the stretcher.

CASTING CALL

JIMMY

The weird thing is the way my mind keeps flashing. Like a disposable camera. Flash. Flash. Flash. And you're blinded by the light. Right? Time freezes. Whatever thought you have, whatever emotion you're feeling, lasts a nanosecond longer than normal.

This is the third "seminar" I have to attend. Between those, AA meetings and community service, I don't have a second to myself. It's a drag, but at least the judge didn't throw me in jail.

The speaker goes on and on and these flashes come at me of moments in my life, like the time Slab held my head under the water in the baby pool and my lungs felt like a balloon before it pops, but the rest of me was calm, peering at the painted fish and sailboats on the bottom. Like the look on Karen's face when she backed down the driveway: so pretty and sad. Then her face when the guys were ribbing her, and the way it made my insides twist like someone wringing a cloth out hard. The same way I felt when Slab pushed the kid off the skateboard.

I have all this *feeling*. I don't want it. The alcohol took it away; that was why I liked it. Maybe that was my mom's problem too. Too much feeling. And Dad's problem is he doesn't have enough of it. Or that it's buried so deep underneath all that military crap that he can't reach it anymore, like a talent you might have that rusts when you don't use it.

He came to bail me out. I was almost sober, in that feeling-like-a-train-just-hit-me way, when he showed up. I was sitting there, still in handcuffs. The cop who was watching me was reading a *Playboy*. He kept holding up the centerfold, opening and closing it. Teasing me. But I didn't give a crap about that naked chick.

I was thinking about Karen, that this latest bit of bad luck was because of the way I'd treated *her*. It didn't make sense, but that was what I was thinking. Those witches, even the plain one, did have some kind of *power*. I'm sure of it. Things got . . . knotted when they were involved. Strange.

I was wishing that Karen was here. She would've made me feel okay. It was funny that I didn't wish for Yvonne. I have this lucky fortune from a fortune cookie. It says, *Everything will go your way in life.* I carry it in my wallet. I figure I'll write her a note and slip it in her locker. The fortune hasn't worked for me; maybe it will work for her.

My dad came in. I guess they'd given him a call. The cop slid the *Playboy* into a drawer and stood up.

Here's the thing. My dad was wearing his army uniform, like he wanted to show the cops that even though his kid was one screwup, he had served his country.

"Dad," I went. He didn't say a word. "Thanks for coming."

No answer.

He didn't speak to me at court either, just listened without a word while the judge gave me probation and rehab. I was so grateful that the judge got it, that it was a prank, not a crime, that I'd just turned eighteen that day, that I didn't need to start my adult life with a felony on my record.

Only on the drive back did we speak. "Does Mom know?" I asked him.

He shrugged. "I called her, but she doesn't answer. She doesn't call me back. So I guess not."

I was starving and shaking. "I'm not going to drink anymore."

"I've heard that before," Dad said. But he meant from my mom; he'd never heard it from me. She'd said it lots, but the funny thing is, she didn't stop drinking until she left *him*. She could only do it for herself, like she said, not for us.

"I'm going to join the army."

He stared straight ahead. My stomach made a loud growl. When I was a kid he'd laugh when my stomach sounded like that.

"I think that's a good idea." Then he pulled into In-N-Out Burger. It was like, for once, he knew what I needed.

The speaker has orange lips and gray hair. She runs a rehab center in the desert. Paying attention to her is part of the trip, of my probation. But my mind keeps on flashing. Even sober, I don't register things the way I'm supposed to.

She says you have to pray and make good decisions for yourself. You have to take care of your life the way you would your car: wash and polish it, fill it with gas.

We all look at her like she's empty space. The guy next to me yawns. The one in front picks at his tattoo, a serpent with a woman's head.

"Think of it this way, then," she says. "Your life is a play. There's a casting call and you make the choice about how to be cast. Do you want to be the hero? The villain? Or the guy who walks on in the first scene and is never heard from again? You decide what happens on the stage."

Life is a play.

And you get to be the author.

CHRISSIE

YVONNE'S SPELL FOR
REKINDLING FRIENDSHIP

Equal parts of loyalty, kindness, generosity, and
forgetfulness (also known as forgiveness). Add
crushed sunflower petals, eucalyptus, mint and
palm fronds. Place in the center of the room and
circle five times. Bake and consume fudge brown-
ies with walnuts and maple frosting. Dance. Sing.
Be silly. Be yourself. Be accepted. No boys shall
come between you.

I had the first real conversation with Jason last night
that I've had in months. He gave me news about different

kids and teachers and even a few animals: Mr. Credenzo still hasn't cut his hair. Dory Abels moved to New York. Wilbur's still doing fine and causing trouble. Only last week, he managed to chew his way into the barn and scare the chickens.

And Morning Glory? I wanted to ask. Instead, I said, "I decided not to go to the poetry workshop after all." Every time I looked at that acceptance letter, my stomach went in knots. Plus, I feel like I'm making progress in creating a life *here*. It seems smart to keep working at it.

He actually sounded disappointed. "I thought I was going to see you."

"You will," I said. "At Christmas. We're coming for the winter break. We're going to stay at the Inn on Lake Champlain."

"Ritzy."

"Yeah. We do things the ritzy way now."

"So I'll get to meet your stepdad?"

"Yeah. Lucky you."

"He sounds nice enough."

"That's what everyone says."

Jason hates it when I whine. It's not what New Englanders do. "How long are you staying?"

"Two weeks. My mom made reservations and everything, so it's a done deal."

"Cool. My dad just started a business in Burlington. We're giving horse-and-carriage rides downtown. You can come along with us."

"Awesome."

"So what are you going to do this summer?"

"There's a science camp at the planetarium. It sounds interesting. And I'll hang out with my friends, Karen and Yvonne."

"It's great you made friends so fast. Maybe I'll come out sometime and meet them."

Another reason I'm staying here for the summer: I feel like Yvonne and Karen need me to help patch things up. Since that day last week when she was taken to the hospital, Karen has spoken to me, but not to Yvonne. I told her that Yvonne didn't do anything with Jimmy and that it's not her fault that Jimmy liked her.

"That's not it," Karen said.

"Then what?" I almost said, *What now?*

"I feel so ashamed of myself. I've betrayed the coven."

"No. You haven't."

"Yvonne must hate me."

"She doesn't."

Finally, I talked her into going to Sanctuary with me to take a yoga class. It wasn't until she agreed that I told her Yvonne would be going too.

"Earth to Chrissie," Mom says. "Which is Karen's house? As many times as I've been here, I forget the way."

"Huh?" My mom bought an SUV. It's a gas hog, but we can all fit in.

"Dreaming poems?" Max says. He is so obnoxious.

"No, dollar signs."

"You stole my dream," he says.

I can't even insult him effectively. "Turn left on the next street."

"This isn't her street?" Mom says.

"No."

"I thought I knew the way. I get so confused driving here."

"That's because everything looks the same," I complain.

"Woody Allen says that the only cultural advantage to living in Los Angeles is that you can turn right on a red light," Max jokes.

"I don't know why you wouldn't let us walk, Mom. It's like two miles. That's nothing."

"I need to know where you are at all times. That's what any good parent of a teen does."

"You call my cell twenty times a day. You were never strict in Vermont."

"You were always with me there. And I'm strict because I've been your age. I got in scrapes. Believe you me. Those Southern boys are all manners until you're alone with them. I remember one dance. Everything I had was passed down from my cousins through Cherry. The dress had a stain across the back of it. Yellow, like a dog had lifted its leg on the thing. I had to sew a pleat in it by hand to cover it. It took me hours. The boy who took me to the dance . . . what was his name? Jeb. He *yes-ma'amed* my parents until they shoved us out the door just to get rid of him. But as soon as he got me in the car, he was all over me. I had to struggle with him so much the pleat ripped out of my dress. I couldn't even go to the dance."

"I've only heard that story ten times." *Okay, maybe once.*

"I've never told you that story."

"Turn right." She practically drives over the curb.

"It's very rude to say you've heard a story before. Even if you have, which you haven't, you can pretend you didn't. My point is, I certainly didn't have my own room, daily cappuccinos or a cell phone."

"They weren't invented yet."

"Or a new car."

"I haven't gotten that yet," I say.

"When have I ever not kept a promise to you?"

I open my mouth to answer, but she reads my mind.

"I said I would do *anything* to make this move right for you. And I have. It's not my fault *anything* isn't enough." The way her voice quivers makes my eyes smart.

"It's getting better, Mom."

"You hear that!" Max chimes in. "Better is a good start. It's a step to best."

"Here's her house."

"Thank God. Cute boy," Mom says. "That's her brother?"

"No, just the housepainter."

Karen runs out. She waves at Troy, who watches her all the way to the car.

"Such a nice girl," Mom says, which means *normal.* Unlike Yvonne.

"Hi, Mr. and Mrs. Morse." Karen climbs in. "Is that right or did you keep your name?"

"That's right. I took Max's name. But call me Ava."

"Nice car."

"It only took seven weeks to pick it out," Max says.

"I wanted a big car that drove like a little car," Mom explains.

"It's a BMW that drives like a BMW." Max thinks he is so funny.

"You won't believe it, Chrissie." Karen squeezes my arm. "I finally told my mom I don't like pink. And she said I could redo my whole room. I'm going to get that futon in the window of Truly Yours, then we're going to Pier One for accessories. She said you could come."

"Cool."

"We did the advertising for Truly Yours," Max says. "That kangaroo under the wicker umbrella. I had to fly to Australia to film that."

"Wow, that's amazing, Mr. Morse. What a great advertisement."

"Now, this building is unmistakable." Mom pulls up in front of Yvonne's apartment. The sign's no longer there, at least. Her dad made her take it down. Mom honks the horn.

"I'll get her," I say, but Yvonne emerges wearing black from head to toe.

"I believe that's what they call Goth," Max says.

"Those are my sunglasses." Mom turns around and gives me this your-friend-is-a-thief look.

"I sort of gave them to her one day. Sorry."

Yvonne opens the door and slides in.

Karen turns and looks away, out the window. Neither of them says anything to the other.

"Hot day, isn't it?" Max says.

No one answers.

The short drive to Sanctuary feels a lot longer with no one speaking. Max gives me a questioning look a couple of times; I act like I don't notice.

We pull up. Yvonne jumps out of the car and walks toward the entrance without us. "Have fun!" Max says. "We'll be in that Japanese place across the street, so just come over if we're not here when you finish."

"Okay. Thanks."

"Yvonne hates me," Karen whispers as we follow Yvonne.

"She doesn't. It'll be okay."

We walk into the cool green entryway. There are green walls, ferns and bamboo, and no sound except the tinkling of a small fountain. I'm glad to be in the silent space, since Yvonne and Karen aren't talking. It makes everything less weird.

We're running late, so we don't have tea. Instead we go straight into the studio, take off our shoes and line them up at the edge of the tatami. There are only three yoga mats left in the room, one across and two next to each other. I rush to the single mat so that Yvonne and Karen will have to be together.

Sensei welcomes us and gives a short talk about letting go of thoughts, of expectations, of anger and of worry. It occurs to me that maybe that's why Max is so pleasant all the time; he's been doing yoga for years.

Sensei bows; then she rings the small gong. Karen giggles. Yvonne cracks a smile but doesn't look at Karen. Then Sensei moves to the center of the room. Her body and movements are those of a ballerina, which is what she used to be. We begin.

When I first started doing the yoga and meditation, my thoughts would run wild. Sensei calls this monkey mind: your thoughts leaping from limb to limb like a monkey in a cage. I would obsess about Jason, my mom and the way my poetry seemed to go downhill since I moved here.

Now whenever I get into the room, my mind slows and I'm able to just be here.

We move through all the postures. The only sound is breathing. At first, I watch Karen and Yvonne. Yvonne picks it up easily. Karen struggles with the positions and keeps glancing over at Yvonne. Gradually, I let go. That's what yoga feels like: letting go of tension and floating with and above your own self.

Sensei rings the gong. Then we sit cross-legged and meditate. Lately, the image of the seagull comes to me when I meditate. But today as my mind relaxes, I drift to Vermont this winter, the streets of Burlington, a horse and carriage. And in this moment, I truly am there and here, all at once. When the gong is rung, I stay in meditation a couple of minutes. I don't want to leave.

When I finally open my eyes, I see Yvonne and Karen, their heads together like best friends. Whispering. Yvonne hates to follow the rules.

YVONNE

SPELL TO LET GO OF THE PAST

Take a strong plant. Lace your fingers around the stem, palm up. With 'all your strength, pull it out of the soil, taking all the roots. Say, "I have taken the roots. You are free to go. To invent yourself. To grow and grow." Then replant it in a different place, water and tend it until it flourishes.

You ever have this feeling that your life is a movie and you're watching it? I think we feel that way when something terrible is happening: when a building is toppling, when a war has begun for no reason (is there ever a reason?), when the wrong President is elected.

Or like that day Karen and Gina drove up and Karen didn't want to be my friend.

"Did you pack your bathing suit?" Dad turns off the freeway.

"Yeah."

"Sunblock?"

"*You* packed it."

"Oh yeah."

"Why are you asking about these things now? We're, like, two hours from home."

"We can stop and buy things."

"Dad, calm down."

"She's going to steal you."

"I won't let her. I'm not four."

"She's gonna pull something."

"I can handle it, Dad."

"Look at those signs." Dad points to a silhouette of a woman dragging a child behind her, a warning that illegal immigrants chased by border police can pop out of cars and run across the freeway at any point. "Those are the people Morgana works with."

"Dad."

"I jumped through all of the hoops to become a citizen."

"You weren't from Mexico. You know it's harder for them."

"If she pulls anything, I'll have her arrested and deported."

"I'm just going to spend a few hours with her and

tell her I'm not staying, then you and I will have our vacation."

"She's very persuasive."

"You think that anyone could talk me out of having a cool vacation in San Diego? I mean, we've *never* had a vacation."

"I know. I'm sorry."

"It's fine. I'm trying to reassure you."

"Why couldn't you meet in a restaurant or a coffee shop? Why do you insist on going *there*?"

"I want to see. I want to know what she's doing and how she lives." The truth is, I'm almost as scared as he is. But having him vent my feelings makes me a little less so.

"Don't let her talk you into staying. I feel for the illegal immigrants too. But I didn't raise you to break the law. You want to help people? Fine. Get a degree in social work or medicine. Work within the system, within the law. I didn't raise you to be a criminal."

"Dad."

"Do you know how much money I have saved for you? For college? Almost a hundred thousand dollars. Hah! You think we're poor and that you'll never get anywhere. . . ."

"I don't think that."

"Well, that's what I've been doing. For your future."

"Boy, you get really crazy around the subject of

Morgana, don't you? I've never heard you string so many sentences together at once."

He sighs. "Yeah. She drives me crazy."

I nod. "And?"

"I loved her."

"And?"

"It wasn't much fun."

"And?"

"I hate her. More. I hate her more than I loved her."

I pat his hand. "Don't worry."

"Don't breathe," he jokes.

"Turn up ahead, Dad. That's it. Then press the odometer. It's point-eight miles, then a dirt road."

"A dirt road! Naturally, it's a dirt road."

"Then you take a quick right and left and park in the first clearing."

"How will I find my way back?"

"Sprinkle breadcrumbs."

"The birds eat those. I should know. Who read you that story every night?"

"You did. Toss stones, then."

"Stop humoring me."

"I've never seen you like this."

"Here it is. A clearing." He turns off the car. "I have a present for you."

"What?"

Dad pulls a cell phone out of his pocket. "You only have a hundred minutes a month."

"Cool."

"Do you know how to work it?"

"Yeah, I use Chrissie's and Karen's all the time."

"Call me as soon as you are done talking to her. My number is programmed here, where it says *Dad*. If I don't hear from you within an hour, I am coming back here."

"Give me three."

"What?"

"Three hours. I haven't seen her for practically my whole life, Dad."

"I'll call the police. If you're not here, I'll call the police."

"Okay, chill. Just drive into Encinitas and have a smoothie or something. Take a walk or see a movie."

"Yeah. Right."

"You sound really lame when you try to talk like a teenager."

"Right."

"Okay." I kiss him, my security blanket, and head on the path to the unknown, which leads up into the hills and curves jaggedly.

It's a small climb but feels like a huge adventure to me. I've done so little in my life. But next year I'll be a junior. I'll have to think about colleges and the future, maybe travel.

Every now and then I see a rock with yellow paint on it, a sign that I'm going the right way.

Karen wanted to come. I should've let her. I don't

know why I felt like I had to meet Morgana on my own. A wish that she'll turn into the mother of my dreams? That she'll be different without my dad there? That's probably true. They both get crazy around each other.

Gradually, as I walk, I hear footsteps behind me, and someone breathing heavily. I step behind a tree and wait, the cell phone in my hand, my heart pounding.

I have this image of illegal aliens as being friendly Mexican guys, like the ones who get hauled off buses in Santa Monica and sent back to the border. They're always so obedient, resigned, when the officers take them off.

The steps come faster. "Dad!"

He jumps. "You just gave me a heart attack."

"What are you doing?"

"I'm taking a walk. Like you said."

"You're following me. You said I could be alone with her."

"Fine. Fine. I'm just trying to look out for you."

"You're trying to . . . to not let me grow up."

"Isn't that a double negative?"

"I'm going by myself. I don't need a fistfight between you two."

"Okay. Swell." Dad turns and walks slowly down the hill.

I wait until I can't hear his footsteps anymore, then I keep going, but I hope a teeny bit that he does stay close by. In a couple of minutes I come to a clearing and a bunch of makeshift tents. There's a laundry line stretching across the whole place, covered in clothes. I wonder if this camp reminds Morgana of life with the Gypsies. We lived in camps like this.

A Mexican woman comes up to me. "Morgana?" she asks, and points.

The tents are erected in a circle. In the middle of it, two women are starting a fire. Morgana appears. Her hair is up on her head, like I wear mine sometimes. She's wearing the same jeans and shoes as the last times I've seen her. At least she has a different shirt. She motions me over to a large lean-to, where a woman lies on a blanket on the ground, rolling in agony. "Is she in labor?" I ask.

"She's not on vacation." Morgana kneels next to her. "She's been in labor since yesterday morning. I've been up all night. Her name is Nola. Have you come to stay? Where are your things?"

I don't answer. Nola begins to moan.

"She's having contractions. They come in waves." Morgana sings to her in Spanish.

I know that I should be sympathetic to Nola and awed by birth. But all I feel is annoyed that I've come here to talk to Morgana and her attention is on the woman, not me.

Finally, Nola's body relaxes and Morgana turns toward me. "Get me that cloth, so I can put it on her head."

"They knew I was here for you," I say as I hand her the cloth. "Did you tell them I was coming?"

"How would I know when you were coming? You look like me. That's why."

Morgana's teeth are crooked, and discolored from smoking. She has dark circles under her eyes. Her hair is like mine, but threaded with gray. I sure hope I look better than her. "What did you do when you found out I was missing?"

"You get to the point, don't you?"

"Yes."

"Massage her feet. It brings on labor."

"I don't want to massage her feet. I don't even know her."

"You're a bad sport." Morgana frowns. "Do you know that? I'll bet you cheat when you play games."

"Why didn't you look harder for me? You could've found me."

"I looked . . . for a while."

"What? Five minutes?"

Morgana massages Nola's feet. "Did you just come here to ask me questions? Like I'm a criminal?"

"I have a right to."

Nola begins to moan again. Morgana looks at her watch. "We're almost there."

"When do *we* get to talk?"

"When she's born. It will be soon."

"She?"

"It will be a girl. I can feel it. What is there to talk about? The past?"

"Yes."

Nola squirms in agony. From behind the tent, a man tiptoes over, his hat in his hands. Morgana says something to him in Spanish. He nods and retreats. Finally, Nola relaxes again.

"Two minutes apart," Morgana says. "Does your dad still play the guitar?"

"I've had to study witchcraft on my own."

"Does he have a girlfriend?"

"Dad says you were one of the most powerful witches among the Gypsies."

"Powerful witch." She spits the phrase back at me. "You become a witch precisely because you *don't* have power."

I try to take that in. "I came to tell you that I'm not coming to be with you this summer. I'm staying with Dad."

Morgana glares. "You are going to learn nothing from me. I have things to pass on, and you are my daughter."

Nola screams something in Spanish and begins to writhe again.

"Muy Pronto," Morgana tells her. *"Casi tiempo."*

I look at poor Nola, giving birth on the ground without anything to help her with the pain, without the choice of that, because she's illegal. A bit of feeling seeps into me. I don't want it to. I want to stay angry at Morgana, the bad witch, the bad mother, with her crowlike face, her cunning eyes, nothing like the mother of my dreams, who tucked me in at night and came to school to volunteer in the classroom.

"This is going on too long," Morgana whispers. "Nola is getting worn out."

"Do a spell."

"Spells are just words. Like prayers and songs. The power is within. You can walk into a room with people, a party, and it can feel like a wonderful place. Or you can go into a room and feel hate and anger. That is because of people's thoughts. I don't want to have power, you know? I don't want to be in control. To be a big shot. Nothing worked when I was trying to be in control."

Nola relaxes again, seems to sleep. She doesn't look much older than me. Morgana strokes Nola's hair. A memory flashes of her touching me like that when I was a child. Is it real?

"That's better," Morgana says. "Now I'm a midwife, the closest thing to being a witch I can think of, but it's still out of my control. The baby's been forming for nine months. But things can go wrong. Women have died in my arms. Babies have come out stillborn. I have delivered them, then dug their graves. I try to help, but it's out of my control. Up to God . . . or whoever."

"How could you have let Dad take me?" I yell.

"Quiet! Don't you dare disturb her." Morgana wipes sweat from her face. "I didn't *let* him. He just did it. I was . . . putting my energy into the wrong things. Into men. Into love."

"But what about me?"

"I wasn't a very good mother," she says. "Okay? He was right. I was a bad mother, and he was right to take you. The life of a Gypsy is no life for a child. Being an outsider, traveling from place to place. Begging from tourists. Being attacked and hated and thrown in jail. Living like this." She gestures around her. "You'll go to college and make something of yourself and not be like me. Do you know where I worked last year? Burger Magic. Frying burgers. I couldn't even work at Burger King! They don't hire illegals. That's right. I'm an illegal too. Like her. Every time the boss walked by he patted me on the ass. And there was nothing I could do about it."

A seed of pity for her works its way in and plants itself. "You could become a citizen or open your own business. Dad does pretty well with the hot dog stand."

"Hot dogs. *Phah*. The smell of them makes me puke." She examines Nola. "I'm so tired today. It must be the heat. Ciella. Yvonne, go drink some water. You don't want to get dehydrated. There's a bottle in my tent. It's the gray one at the back attached to that oak. Water is the main challenge out here."

I look around. Everything is brown; drought conditions. I always think of our apartment as crummy, but this puts things in perspective. "Do you want some?"

"No. I'll have to pee then, and I can't leave. She's almost there."

As I walk to her tent, I sense Dad's presence. I turn around, looking, but don't see him. I check the cell phone. Inside the tent are a beat-up sleeping bag, a small vase with flowers, and a note: *Lovely Lady,* it says. *Gracias.* This is Morgana's home, where she wants me to spend my summer. As I leave the tent, I hear rustling in the leaves. I don't even have to look to know it's Dad, his big footsteps. I ignore him.

I bring Morgana water. "Have some."

She takes a sip. "I was looking forward to you staying." An admission.

My heart softens. "I'll see you back in L.A.," I promise. "You'll be back there, won't you?"

She nods.

It's true, I know. I will see her again. In whatever form, my mother is here to stay.

Nola cries out.

"The baby is coming," Morgana whispers. "Go ask one of the men for hot water. Say, *'Agua caliente:'* Go!"

I run to the center of camp, where the pot of water is boiling on the fire. *"¡Agua!"*

Two men take either side of the pot and bring it to my mother. I trail behind.

"*¡Empaja, Nola!*" Morgana urges. "Push!" The baby's head and neck are already out. I stare, frozen, at the dark head of hair, the red face.

The baby slips out suddenly into Morgana's arms. And it *is* a girl, shrieking for all she's worth, making sure the world takes notice of her.

CHRISSIE

In the beginning
was the word.
And the word had
two syllables.
Water.

Summer, finally. No more bad English class. No more overcrowded halls and noisy cafeteria.

It's about a hundred degrees. The sand is so scorching I had to run across it to get to the wet, cool part. The sky is amazing, completely blue with clouds so fluffy they look like they're out of a picture book. The water is bright and clear.

"What are you thinking?" Karen asks.

"Me?" I say.

"You were just staring off into space."

"She's always thinking," Yvonne says. Mom let Yvonne keep the Dior glasses. They look great on her.

"About Sam's party?" Karen asks.

I laugh. "No. Although he was so nice, the way he asked. He said, 'Your parents can talk to my parents if they're nervous.' And he told me to bring anyone I wanted. That means you guys."

"And Gina?" Karen says.

"Sure."

"We're getting popular because of you, Chrissie," Yvonne jokes. She's finally accepted letting Gina hang with us sometimes.

"Yeah. Right."

"So your mom said yes?" Karen asks.

"*Max* said yes, but he gave me this big lecture on boys that age."

"That's sweet," Karen says.

"It is?" I have to admit Max bugs me less lately.

"He's acting like a dad."

"Max is a good person," Yvonne muses. "He's just got different values than us."

"No kidding. You know what he said the other day? He goes, 'There are two kinds of people—people with taste, and people who drink white zinfandel.' "

"What is white zinfandel?" Karen asks.

"Pink wine. He's such a snob."

"It's your mom you're really mad at," Yvonne says.

"I guess."

"And maybe even your dad."

"Nah," I say, but a spurt of anger does bubble up. *Why did Dad have to be away so much, and doing dangerous things? Someone who worked for him could have been climbing out on the pipe, someone younger and more limber and used to doing things like that.* But as soon as that anger comes, reason returns. *Because my dad wasn't the type of man to let someone else do the dirty work. He would have wanted to check the engineering and test the system himself.* "You know, what I never realized is that my mom was never happy in Vermont. I mean, I think she loved my dad so she put up with it. But she hated living in the woods and him being gone all the time. Even when he was home, he and I would be skiing and snowshoeing and sapping maples. She was pretty much left out."

"Is she happier with Max?" Yvonne asks.

"Yeah, when I think about it. She's happier."

"But you're not."

I shrug. A family of sandpipers dashes through the water in front of us.

"I'm mad at *my* dad too," Karen says.

"Why?" Yvonne asks.

"He pays more attention to the housepainter than to me."

"The housepainter pays more attention to *you,* though," I say.

"He does talk to me a lot. He asked me if I like musicals. Then he said there was a musical, *Wicked,* coming to the Shubert."

"What will you do if he asks you?" I say.

"I think I'll go. I mean, he seems nice, so I should give it a chance. He practically lives at my house anyway."

Yvonne whistles. "A college boy."

"Anyway, I'm cured about Jimmy. I did that spell from your book, the one for the brokenhearted."

"How does it go?" I ask.

"*Stars are struck. Moons are beams. The cure for love is what it seems. The doe will find another buck. To replace the one who has no luck.*"

"Maybe Troy's that buck," I joke.

"You know . . ." Karen's face gets serious. "When I thought I might be pregnant, I realized that I do want a family someday. That means I need to be with a boy who's responsible and successful, not one who gets drunk and tries to hold up a bank."

"He didn't hold up a bank." Yvonne smiles. "He just tried to pry open the ATM."

"That's pretty bad," I say.

"Did you talk to him?" Karen asks. "I don't mind if you did. Really."

"He talked to *me,*" Yvonne admits. "He told me he's going to AA. He tried to join the army, but because he's on probation for a felony, they wouldn't take him."

"I thought they'd take anyone," I say.

"I told him, 'Consider it a message from the Fates.' That was the conversation. He's a decent kid underneath it all. I mean, that's the thing. He is a kid."

"Well, I'll never *get* Jimmy," I say.

"I'm glad he didn't go into the army." Karen shudders. "Hey, you know something? The last day of school someone put a fortune in my locker . . . from a fortune cookie. It said *You will have a good life.* But on the other side, they had written SORRY in big letters."

"You didn't tell us about that," Yvonne says.

"I figured it was from Slab, so I flushed it down the toilet."

"You'll still get to have a good life," Yvonne says. "You don't have to keep a fortune for it to work."

"Yeah." Karen tugs at her hair. She can't stand to think about Slab or the test she had to take for HIV. Thank God: it came back negative.

"Maybe it was from Jimmy," I say.

"I was just thinking that same thing," Karen says. "All of a sudden I got that *feeling.*"

The tide changes. The water inches closer. I step back.

"So . . . what were *you* thinking about, Chrissie," Yvonne asks, "when this whole conversation started?"

"That." I point. "It's so big."

"It's the ocean," Karen laughs.

"Don't remind me."

"You know how to swim," Yvonne says. "You said so yourself."

"That was in a pool."

"Pretend this is a pool, then."

"Pools don't have waves."

"Yvonne and I will hold you," Karen says. "Then you'll feel safe."

"Have you heard from your mom?" I change the subject.

"Yeah," Yvonne says. "She finally called again. She keeps bugging me to come back and stay with her. She goes, 'Here is a list of what you should bring.' "

"Does she talk like that?" Karen asks.

"Like what?"

"Like Count Dracula. You sound like Count Dracula when you imitate her."

"She's Romanian. I'm not good at accents. Her English is good, though."

"You're not going to stay with her. Are you?" I ask. After I stayed home instead of going to Vermont, I'd be bummed if she took off.

"My dad would freak if I did. It's just . . . the work she's doing. It seems important. I can't believe I watched a baby being born."

"That must've been awesome," I say.

"And she must be lonely."

"But . . . ," Karen says.

"But what?" Yvonne smiles.

"She doesn't sound very nice."

"She's not. I'm glad my dad stole me from her. I've

spent my whole life being mad about it, but now I think he probably did the right thing."

"We should scry. That will tell you what to do," Karen says.

"What's that?" I ask.

"Ah, there's still so much to learn." Yvonne pats my head. "Scrying is looking in a bowl of water for guidance from the universe. Watch." She runs up on the beach and comes back with a bucket.

"Whose is that?" Karen asks.

"Some kid's, I guess. It was just there because I needed it. I'll bring it back when I'm done." Yvonne walks into the surf and fills it, then kneels in the sand and peers into the bucket. "You're supposed to do this with clear water . . ." Yvonne makes circles with the bucket and stares into it.

"Does it always take this long?" I whisper to Karen. She nods.

"Shall I go with my mother?" Yvonne asks of the water.

Karen crosses her fingers and shakes her head at me.

"What do you see?" I say.

"A lot of sand floating around. A small world of beach and ocean."

"How does it work? Do words appear in the water, or what?"

"The water's a focal point," Karen explains. Yvonne

has taught her well. "It's like the crystal ball. The image enters your mind."

"I can't do it." Yvonne passes the bucket to me. "I'm not detached. You try it, Chrissie."

"I'm not ready for this." I look in the bucket. Water. Teeming with invisible life.

"You're as ready as you'll ever be."

I take a deep breath and try to be receptive. The water is muddy. I can feel my white shoulders burning under the sun's rays. The smell of coconut oil and salt. "Don't go with your mom. Even if she's doing good work, it doesn't mean she'll be good to you, or that she deserves you. Your dad will be so lonely without you, and so will we." I look back up at them. Karen is smiling.

"Good job," Yvonne says, seriously. "You've become an excellent witch."

"I was just saying how I feel."

"That's half the battle," Karen says.

"Ready to take the plunge?" Yvonne knots her hair on top of her head.

"We can swim off our energy," Karen says, "then we won't be so nervous at the party."

"It's the final step in your apprenticeship," Yvonne coaxes.

"I don't think so."

"You're afraid. It's okay to be afraid," Yvonne says.

"Is it?"

"So long as it doesn't stop you from living your life."

"I knew there was a hitch."

"It's not that easy to drown," Karen says, "especially in the ocean; the salt keeps you afloat."

I think of her being dragged onto the beach by the paramedics, of the water coming out of her mouth.

As if she's read my thoughts, she says, "I thought I was going to drown that day. I didn't realize how far out I was swimming, and it was so cold. But then God sent that surfer to save me, and even better, you guys were there. That was so amazing."

"That's because we're a coven," Yvonne says. "It was synchronicity. We were there when you needed us."

"God will keep you afloat, Chrissie." Karen touches my arm.

"I don't believe in God."

"You don't believe in God?" Yvonne frowns. "And you don't believe in witchcraft. So what do you believe in?"

"Us. I believe in us."

Yvonne takes my hand. She tugs me toward the water. "We are the witches of the sea. . . ."

"Why can't I be a witch, but not of the sea? Why can't I be a witch of the trees or something or of the charming freeways?"

Yvonne stares hard at me. She doesn't look amused. "How did your dad die? Was it the fall?"

"No."

"He drowned?"

"Yeah." The sun shoots rays into my eyes. I pull my sunglasses down.

"In the ocean?" Karen asks.

"No. A river. In India. After he fell, he was okay. He was trying to swim to shore. The other workers rushed down to the bank to help him, but they didn't have a boat. They got tree limbs and stuck them out for him. But the current was strong and he drowned."

The sun ducks behind a cloud. A kid comes rushing up, grabs the bucket, glares at us and runs off.

"I know!" Karen says. "Why doesn't Chrissie just put her feet in, like she can *anoint* her feet in water? Doesn't that sound kind of mystical? Then, next summer, her ankles. By the time we're out of high school, she'll be up to her waist."

"Her feet?" Yvonne frowns.

"Yeah."

"I can put my feet in. No problem." The cloud passes and the day brightens again. Someone turns on a radio. "Where Are You Going?" by Dave Matthews floats across the sand.

"You're missing out," Yvonne says.

"I know. Really I do."

"She knows," Karen echoes.

"Fine," Yvonne says. "Your feet."

I step into the water, dipping my toes into the foam. "Go ahead. I'll watch."

"Run for it, Yvonne!" Karen tugs Yvonne's hand.

My two witches dash, screaming, into the ocean, diving under the waves, stroking until they're so far out that their heads look like two buoys floating and bobbing.

And yeah, it does look fun.

I close my eyes and imagine Vermont. It's humid in the summer. Would Jason have had time for me? What would our old house look like? Would it have changed? I miss it, but if I'd gone, I would also have missed Karen and Yvonne, and Sam's party, and the beach, which I'm starting to enjoy. I open my eyes.

"We are the witches of the sea," I mumble to myself, letting the surf lick up around my ankles, then my calves, the sun reflecting off the glassy water, shimmering in the air like a white flame.

ACKNOWLEDGMENTS

Many thanks to my husband, Michael Ruben; to Jean Brown; to my agent, Michael Bourret; and to Wendy Lamb, Ruth Homberg, Kaitlin McCafferty, Angela Carlino, and Kristen McKeegan of Random House, who helped make this book all it could be.

KELLY EASTON is the author of several young adult novels: *The Life History of a Star, Walking on Air, Aftershock,* and *Hiroshima Dreams,* as well as the Betts Pets series for children. Her stories and books have been singled out for various honors, including a Golden Kite Honor for Fiction from the Society of Children's Book Writers and Illustrators, a Julia Ward Howe Honor, a Book Sense 76 Best Book listing, a Westchester's Choice listing, ALA listings, a North Carolina Writers' Workshop Prize, and the Sojourner Fiction Prize. Kelly Easton is also a teacher. She lives in Rhode Island and on Martha's Vineyard with her husband, Michael Ruben, and their children: Rebecca, Mollie, Isabelle, and Isaac.